MY SISTER'S FLIRTY FRIEND

PIPER RAYNE

Cover Design: By Hang Le

Cover Photo: Wander Aguiar Photography

1st Line Editor: Joy Editing

2nd Line Editor: My Brother's Editor

Proofreader: My Brother's Editor

About My Sister's Flirty Friend

I broke the cardinal rule and slept with my sister's best friend.

Granted, I'd just found out that I was now a single father to a three-year-old little girl and was low on willpower.

It should also be noted that there's been sexual tension between us for years. There's no way it would be a surprise if anyone in our small town found out. That is if we were telling people, which we're not.

We're in agreement to keep our affair a secret, especially since neither one of us do relationships.

You've probably figured it out already, but things didn't go as planned.

my sister's flirty
FRIEND

<u>**The Greenes**</u>

<u>**Hank's Kids**</u>
Cade Greene (33)
Co-owner Truth or Dare Brewery
Fisher Greene (31)
Sheriff
Xavier Greene (29)
Pro Football Player
Adam Greene (27)
Forest Ranger
Chevelle Greene (26)
Water Boat Tourist

<u>**Marla's Kids**</u>
Jed Greene (33)
Co-owner of Truth or Dare Brewery
Nikki Greene (30)
Radio Host
Mandi Greene (28)
Owner of SunBay Inn
Posey Greene (24)
Owner of Fringe

<u>**Hank and Marla's Kid**</u>
Rylan Greene (13)

Chapter One

Jed

"Jed, I need some help out here!" Molly calls from the hallway then knocks on my office door.

I stop what I'm doing and don't mind a bit. I'm working on the business end of running a successful brewery. My stepbrother, Cade, usually handles all things paperwork, but he's asked me to take over some of his tasks while he plans his perfect wedding with his fiancée, Presley.

Since we began this business venture after college, he's handled the business and I've handled the beer making and staff, so I forgot how much I loathe this shit. Plus, I *am* the personality of the bar, so I should be out in front of customers.

No offense to Cade. People love him. He's lived in this town his whole life while I've only been here since I was a senior in high school. My mom married his dad—which is a whole other story—and we went from being enemies to friends to brothers. I love the guy, but his wedding is becoming way too much, if you ask me.

I open my office door and trudge down the hall. Sure enough, the brewery has filled up pretty fast. I should've expected as much since it's the last day before tourist season begins in our small town of Sunrise Bay, Alaska. I'm surprised Molly didn't bang on the door sooner.

She's working behind the bar, dressed in fitted black jeans that are frayed in certain places, along with her Truth or Dare Brewery T-shirt that always fits a little snug, especially in the chest area. I shouldn't notice because Molly is my sister Nikki's best friend. Nikki would gouge out my eyes if she knew the thoughts that go through my head sometimes when Molly's around.

But she looks so damn good all the time and she flirts with me, so it's not like I'm alone in my thoughts. But then again, that's Molly. She's been the town flirt as long as I've known her.

"About fucking time," she grumbles, passing me to grab a can of our new hard seltzer. She cracks it open and passes it to a blonde waiting at the bar.

"There's a lot of office shit to do, and once again, Cade is MIA." I take a man's order and pass him a beer.

"He's getting married."

"And we all know how I feel about marriage."

The two of us continue serving the bar that's now three deep while the serving staff takes care of the customers at tables. I really should've scheduled more help for us tonight. Cade said he'd be late, but I didn't think he meant this late.

It's usually a Greene family tradition that everyone in our family finds their way here the night before tourist season starts up.

Nikki elbows her way through the crowd, stealing a stool right before George from Handyman Haven was going to sit down. "I'm exhausted."

"Sorry." Her husband, Logan, comes behind her, apologizing to everyone as they eyeball Nikki. "Pregnancy."

Nikki rolls her eyes. "Do not apologize for me. I'm

carrying around a damn watermelon and you thought it'd be romantic to walk around the bay."

Molly laughs and slides a water to her. "How are you holding up?"

Nikki looks blankly at her. "How does it look? If people thought I was a bitch before, they're going to think I'm Cruella de Vil before this baby pops out."

"Stop being a bitch then," I say, taking an order from a group of women. They each take turns looking me up and down with a flirtatious smile. What can I say? I am a ladies' man.

"Watch it, Jed," Nikki warns, but I'm too busy filling the women's orders to worry about her idle threat.

"Seriously, she's on the verge of getting in the ring with anyone who crosses her." Logan's eyes widen in an expression that says to take him seriously.

"Speaking of…" I take the credit card from the woman paying for the round of drinks and cash her out while talking to Logan and Nikki. "Fisher and I are having a fight night at our place Sunday night."

"Why?" Nikki's forehead scrunches up. "Logan's not fighting anymore."

"It's a good excuse for us all to get together." I shrug and pass the woman back her card.

Nikki's eyebrows rise. I don't blame her. Who would've thought I'd want the entire family over at my place? Usually the only good thing that comes from it is that my mom cleans the house. But ever since three of the siblings in our blended family have found their one and only, I've started to feel our family's deep-sewn threads tug in different directions.

"Okkaaayyy." Nikki glances at Molly, who only shrugs and continues to serve customers.

"Are you judging me?" I slide by Molly.

In the time she's worked here, we've perfected how to work together behind the bar. Sliding past one another without bumping into each other because we always seem to be aware of the other's proximity, keeping an ear out for what a customer wants and passing the other a beer from the fridge if we're the one who's closer. Hell, we've even perfected the flirtatious vibe between us—all without ever crossing the line.

We've come close though. Last year, Molly caught me beating off in the office. I know, unprofessional as hell, but if you'd seen how good she looked that day, you'd understand. I couldn't wait until I got home for a release if I didn't want to do something stupid with her. Our eyes locked for a moment when she busted into the office—hers wide with shock and surprise and mine at half-mast with lust. I know I would've had a moment of weakness if she had stepped inside, but she didn't. She shut the door with a yelp. I said, "I know it's big but it's not that scary"—after I finished and left the office, of course.

She razzed me about it not being big and how she probably couldn't find it with a microscope and a pair of tweezers. I laughed because I appreciate humor, especially in an uncomfortable situation.

Sometime during the next half hour of making sure everyone is served, the rest of the Greenes trickle in, finding their way to a table that Nikki is now protecting as if the chairs are her cubs. She's definitely not one of those glowing pregnant women you hear about.

When Cade comes in, I groan. "Finally."

He glances at me and kisses Presley on the cheek before pulling out her chair. "I told you I was going to be late."

"And now we have to give Molly a raise," I say.

"Oh, I like the sound of this," she chirps, pouring beers for a group of guys huddled together at the end of the bar.

Molly delivers the beers and I watch as, one by one, each guy checks her out. It's clear why. Molly is not the girl next door. She's a bit on the wild side, always up for anything, and her sharp tongue only makes you want to know what she'd say if you were in bed with her. I have my suspicions she's one of those women who will tell you exactly what she wants. Which is a huge turn-on, and if she wasn't my younger sister's best friend, I'd probably have made a move by now.

After she's finished serving them, they tip her. With her back to them, Molly tucks the twenty-dollar bill in her bra.

"What happened to the community pot?" I jiggle the tip jar behind the counter.

"Once you've got a pair of tits that bring in a crisp twenty, I'll be more than happy to split the tips." She smiles and moves over to my family's table.

"Fight night at our house Sunday," I announce to everyone.

"Oh good. I have something big to tell you all then," my mom says.

All of us siblings exchange glances.

My mom grew up in Sunrise Bay but moved to Arizona with my dad after they married. She only returned after the son of a bitch cheated on her and they divorced. It's then she rekindled her feelings for Hank, my dad's cousin, and they were married, blending our families together. The last time she had something big she wanted to share, we were told our little brother Rylan had been conceived. Now I'm not so sure I want to find out what she wants to share with us.

It was another killer night before tourist season. All the townspeople came to the downtown square to enjoy themselves before we're inundated with tourists and we're all working our asses off until fall.

I head to the office in the back to take a look at some numbers and see how we did tonight. Cade was willing to stay, but I told him to go home with Presley. I don't have anything else to do and one of us might as well be screwing someone tonight. Part of the problem with partnering with family is that when they piss you off, you still do what's right, so you don't get the satisfaction of being difficult.

I package up the deposit and drop it in the safe to take to the bank tomorrow morning. The office door creeps open as I'm sitting back in my seat.

"I'm heading out. Everything is all done," Molly says, leaning against the doorframe.

I lean back in my chair and steeple my hands together. "Thanks."

"Are you almost done? I could wait." She saunters in and slides up on my desk, crossing her legs.

God, she looks good. Molly's looked good since the first time I saw her when I arrived in Sunrise Bay. I've wondered a few times what would've transpired if Nikki hadn't claimed Molly as her bestie.

I gesture toward the desk. "I should finish what I was already doing before you couldn't handle the crowd."

She places her hands under her thighs and tilts her head with raised eyebrows, a teasing glint in her eyes. "It's not my fault every guy wants to flirt with me."

"You don't have to flirt back. The last I saw, the sign outside didn't say this was a strip club."

"Jealous?" She smiles, her gaze floating down my body, lingering on the full sleeves of tattoos on my arms.

"Never."

Lie. All lies. I've been jealous of the attention Molly garners. But that's not to say I haven't had my own fun. Sometimes I think we're cut from the same cloth. Neither of us wants a relationship. I've never seen Molly show any interest in anyone past a few dates. She always finds something wrong with the guy.

We sit in my office, our eyes locked for a brief moment, though it feels like an hour as the sexual tension rolls in like a thick fog after a storm.

I clear my throat, breaking her gaze, and she hops down from the desk. "See you later, boss." She pushes her dark hair off her shoulder and eyes me as she exits the room.

"Want me to walk you to your car?"

She stops and coyly glances at me from the doorway. "No worries, I'm a tough girl."

Not moving from my chair, I admire her body as she laughs and walks out. A few seconds later, the sound of the back door opening and shutting echoes down the hall.

Maybe I'm an idiot for not taking the opportunity. I'm pretty sure she's more than willing, and we could definitely hide it from Nikki. As I think of all the reasons why it'd be okay to sleep with Molly, I finally come to my senses—Molly is a fixture in my big family. Like every one of my siblings' friends, my mom has wrapped her in a welcoming blanket as if she's one of our own. There's no way she could be like my usual type—the ones I can fuck and forget—because Molly isn't going anywhere.

And ever since everything went down when I was seventeen, I swore to myself that I won't do strings.

Molly

On Saturday morning, I'm weaving between cars in Anchorage while glancing at the clock on the dash. If I'm late again, Professor Locklear is sure to give me a dressing down in front of the class. I'm the oldest person in my program since I've only been a part-time student since I graduated high school, which is also why I have a class on the damn weekend.

Pulling off the highway, I briefly pause at a red and turn right, barreling down the road until I reach campus. Of course, there are no parking spots in the student parking and my gaze falls to the clock again. Five minutes before class starts. Crossing my fingers the parking service workers somehow miss this part of campus, I pull into a fifteen-minute parking spot, grab my bag, and race to the lecture hall.

The door is closed when I arrive, and when I open it, it's clear Professor Locklear has stopped his lecture because all my classmates turn in my direction. I offer a small wave, walking down the row of chairs, finding my usual seat in the front row still vacant.

"Thank you for joining us, Miss Monroe." Mr. Locklear walks away from his podium to stand in front of me. "We're not keeping you from something, are we?"

The class quietly giggles.

I glance over my shoulder, feeling my cheeks heat. "No. I'm sorry. I—"

He puts his hand up to silence me, and since he's one of the rare people I listen to, I shut my mouth. I respect Professor Locklear and understand his frustration that I'm late more than I am on time.

"See me after class," he says quietly and returns to the podium. "As I was saying…"

He continues his lecture, discussing our clinical work involving speech therapy. This semester, each one of us has a child to work with in a clinical setting with our mentors. With two months to go, I know my little guy, Dillon, will be the star. He's come so far so fast. After living on the Native villages farther north, he was behind because of the lack of resources up there.

I jot down some notes and answer questions because even though I'm late, I'm Professor Locklear's star student. The entire class knows it, although no one I went to high school with would believe it.

Finally, he eyes the clock and tells us all to enjoy the nice spring day, but his gaze meets mine. "Stay back, Miss Monroe."

I pack my bag and slide out of my seat to head over to him. "I'm sorry I'm late, it's just—"

Again he cuts me off. "Although I'm usually entertained by the excuses you come up with, we have a problem we need to discuss. Walk with me to my office."

"Oh, Professor, I'm not sure we're a good match." My joke dies when he glares at me, his sympathetic dark eyes telling me now is not the time.

"What is it?" I ask, my stomach plummeting as though I'm in those gravity rides at the amusement parks. "You're not about to tell me I'm one credit shy in an elective or something? Because I'm going to be thirty this summer and if I do not have my degree by that point, I'm officially declaring myself a loser."

He pushes open the door and we walk down the stained linoleum floor. All I can concentrate on is his long, dark hair pulled back into a ponytail. It's so silky and shiny that I'd normally ask what kind of conditioner he uses, but he's not in the mood for jokes. The longer the silence carries on, the more worried I become.

Professor Locklear is a straight shooter. He tells you how it is and never plays games. Those sympathetic dark eyes mess with me until he opens his office door and stretches his arm for me to go in first.

"Take a seat," he says, shrugging off his suit jacket and hanging it on the coat rack in the corner of his office.

I sit in the same chair I have tons of times before, my knee bouncing as I wait to hear his news. He sits in his office chair and links his hands together as his elbows rest on the chair arms. When I'm about to scream, his eyes lock with mine.

"This is going to be hard to hear, so I'm just going to spit it out. I received a call last night from Dillon's father. They're going back up to the Native villages. Dillon's grandfather has grown ill, and the family needs them up there."

"What?"

He nods. "His decision is final. He wanted me to thank you for everything you've done for Dillon, and he hopes that one day they'll be back down toward Anchorage, but…"

"They screwed me," I say a little too vehemently.

"They did no such thing. Sure, this situation isn't ideal. There's no way you can present the work you've done without finishing the next six weeks, but you'll just have to come back this fall and redo your clinical. You'll graduate in December."

My heart joins my stomach in the pit of despair. "December. I'll be thirty."

"It's only a difference of six months, Molly."

I stare at the floor. The ivory swirls in the brown carpet resemble a maze. Either that or I'm about to faint. With how fast my heart is racing, I wouldn't be surprised. "I've been at this for years. There has to be something you can do. Can't you talk to the dean?" I inch up on the edge of my chair. "Please, Professor."

"Molly, you're still going to graduate. Just not as planned."

"Do you know how long I've waited for this? I'm an octogenarian compared to my classmates."

He tilts his head with an expression that says, "Not true." But while the other students are all at keg parties and sorority meetings, I have no life except for work and school.

"Well, it feels that way. Twelve years, Professor Locklear. I can't wait any longer to start my real life. There has to be something that can be done." A tear trickles down my cheek, but I swipe it away before he sees it. At least I hope I do. "Please. Maybe I can find another child to help."

"You know we have to scrounge for sign-ups every year. Not everyone is good with a student working one on one with their child."

"Can we at least try?" I hate the slight whine in my voice, but I feel as if someone opened up the bottom of the earth and I'm free-falling, frantically waving my arms to grab at anything that can stop me.

He blows out a breath. "You'd have to use what you've done with Dillon and then whatever you do with a new child. And I cannot allow the new child to only have six weeks of your time and send them off. That isn't fair to them."

"Absolutely not. I can continue after the school year ends."

"You'd be able to graduate, but you'd have to do the rest of the work during the summer. I'm teaching a course, so I might be able to see if the dean will grant permission for me to look over your work since I'll be around anyway."

"Please." I put my hands together in prayer pose. "I'll do anything."

He stares at me long and hard. "Like come to class on time every day from here on out?" One of his bushy eyebrows arches.

My shoulders sag. "It's not like I'm deliberately late."

He cocks his other eyebrow.

"Deal. I won't be late again."

"Doubtful." He swivels his head and looks out the window. "Let me talk to Dean Witner and I'll let you know. No promises."

I jump from my chair. "Thank you so much!"

He holds up his hand. "Don't get so excited until you know whether I can make this happen. If it was anyone else—"

"You'd do the same thing," I finish for him, because that's just who Professor Locklear is.

"Probably. Now get out of here while I figure out the best angle to try to convince the dean and where on earth we'll find another child for you to help."

I do a little dance but refrain from hugging him even though I want to. "Thank you again."

He nods and shoos me out the door.

I step outside, shutting his door, and release a breath. If I find a child for the program, how can they keep me from graduating? Looks like I'll be talking to Lucy Greene. She's an elementary school teacher. Surely, she must know a child who would benefit from speech therapy.

Chapter Three

Jed

On Sunday afternoon, everyone is over at Fisher's and my place, watching last night's MMA fight. We would've watched last night, but we were all working. I dump a bag of chips in a bowl and place it on the coffee table, then sit next to my youngest brother, Rylan.

"My baby thanks you for the nourishment." Nikki snags a chip and bites into it.

"Nothing but the best for my niece or nephew." I wink at her and grab the remote since the fight just ended.

"Guys, I've got things to do at the inn. I need to get outta here." Mandi lingers behind the chair where Nikki is sitting on Logan's lap.

Those two are all over each other all the damn time. And now they're whispering to one another. This is how I know I need to get laid, when I find myself jealous of my pregnant sister going home and getting some from her husband.

"Not yet," Nikki says. "Mom said she's coming by with a big announcement."

I would've bet money Logan wanted to get Nikki home already. Those two sneak off every chance they get.

"If she's pregnant, I'm moving in with one of you."

Rylan picks up the controller for my gaming system and I grab my own. So does Fisher.

"She can't be pregnant," I say, glancing at my little brother. I mean, surely she's too old now, right?

"Those two are worse than you and Logan," Xavier says to Nikki. "Like right now."

"Hey, seating is limited. We're doing you all a favor by sharing," Logan says, gripping her hip tighter.

"They'll be saying they have to go soon," Mandi says, and Nikki sticks out her tongue at her.

The door opens and my mom and Hank come inside holding flags and signs that say, "Vote Greene." We all stare as they walk around the room and pass them out. What the hell is going on?

Then my mom pulls out a bag of pins. "Guess what?"

"Dad's running for mayor?" Adam says.

I don't think he's right because Hank is way too busy with his handyman business. Either my mom is recruiting one of us, which wouldn't surprise me, or she's running herself. Sam Klein, Sunrise Bay's mayor, just announced he's retiring after his term is done.

Hank shakes his head and puts up his hands. "Not me."

I knew it.

"Marla is!" Hank raises his hand and she high fives him as though they're a wrestling tag team.

Everyone looks too stunned to say anything.

My mom beams. "That's right. I've decided to run for mayor."

"Why?" Mandi stares at her flag with distaste. "Don't you have enough to do?"

"You don't look happy." Mom's smile fades as she looks around the room. "None of you do."

Hank shifts behind Mom and glares at us over her head.

We all force smiles.

"Awesome," I say, splashing on a wide grin. "We'll hang a sign in the brewery."

"I can put one up at Fringe," Posey pipes up. "What else do you need help with? I could be your campaign manager. Or you could run your office out of Fringe."

"Suck-up," Fisher coughs out.

Posey is always Mom's biggest cheerleader. The two of them used to go to craft fairs and farmers' markets, where Mom sold her salad dressings. Posey is probably the best salesperson out of all of us, which I'm sure she got from my dad's side. Everyone knows he can sell anything to anyone.

"You'll all play a part in getting your mom elected, so put your thinking caps on," Hank says with authority.

"As though my life wasn't embarrassing enough." Rylan groans and sinks into the couch.

I ruffle his hair. "Hey, maybe this will earn you points with the girls."

Of course it won't. It's hard enough being a Greene in this town, let alone your mom being the mayor.

Someone knocks on the front door, and we all look at one another for a beat, wondering who it could be. Most of us are here, and those who aren't here wouldn't bother to knock. Fisher groans and puts down the controller, rising from the couch to open the door. A man dressed in a suit and holding a briefcase stands there.

"Did someone die?" Rylan asks Mom.

She and Hank walk toward the door.

"I'm looking for Jed Greene," the man says.

Mom, Hank, and Fisher all turn and glare at me. I

continue playing *Mario Kart* because I'm on the last lap and about to win.

"Jed," Mom says with a tone of disapproval, since I'm not Johnny on the spot to find out what this guy wants. It's Sunday afternoon—he's probably selling something. "This man is here to see you."

I look up and drop the controller, annoyed to end the game just to hear some guy give me a crappy sales pitch for new windows or some shit.

Lucy, Chevelle, and Cam come into the room from the kitchen, undoubtedly curious to see who rang the doorbell.

"I'm Jed," I say, sticking my hands into the pockets of my jeans.

"Would you like to talk outside?" the man asks, gesturing to the door.

I glance back at my family and laugh. "Nah, I've got nothing to hide."

Let's be honest, even if I did step outside, every other Greene would have their ears pressed to the door anyway. We don't really respect family members' secrets around here.

"We mailed you a letter and tried to call the number we had listed for you, but since this is a time-sensitive matter, I agreed to come out here personally. I was a friend of my client."

I can't piece together what he could be talking about, but the client bit makes me a little wary. My forehead creases and I cross my arms, widening my stance. "Time-sensitive?"

"You didn't open your mail?" Mom scolds from behind me.

My gaze detours to the oversized pile of unopened mail on the table by the front door. So sue us. Fisher and I are bachelors and everything is done electronically now.

"I've been busy," I say to my mom.

"My name is David Webb. I'm a lawyer and a friend of Tanya Eaton."

I nod slowly. "Okay…"

"Do you remember Tanya Eaton?" Mr. Webb asks.

"Oh, the day has finally arrived," Mandi says.

"What are you talking about?" Nikki whispers to Mandi, louder than she should.

But the lawyer beats Mandi to the punch. "Unfortunately, Miss Eaton passed a few weeks ago from a severe asthma attack."

"Oh," Mom sighs.

"I'm sorry to hear that, but I don't know a Tanya Eaton." I glance over my shoulder at my mom, who has her hand over her heart as though she knew the woman.

"About four years ago, you and Miss Eaton had… relations."

My siblings all laugh at that word. I'm with them. Just say we screwed. Still not sure why this guy is on my doorstep telling me all this though. I don't remember this Tanya Eaton and I feel badly that she passed, but I'm sure she didn't leave me anything in her will.

Mom and Hank quiet the group.

David Webb continues without a word from me. "Those relations resulted in the conception of a little girl. Tan—Miss Eaton—has named you as the little girl's father, and according to her will, she wants you to have sole custody. She has no other living relatives."

All feeling leaves my body. "What?" I whisper, my arms dropping to my sides.

There's no way. I've always used protection. *Always.* And contrary to popular belief, I actually don't sleep with so many women that I wouldn't remember their names.

"But first you need to come down to Minnesota and take a paternity test."

"This can't be right. I don't know this woman." Now that the feeling is back in my body, I shake my head.

"Here." Mr. Webb reaches into his jacket pocket and pulls out a picture. "This is Tanya and… the little girl."

Before my fingers grip the picture fully, the girl's eyes stare back at me and my lungs squeeze, making it hard to breathe. My family rushes up behind me, straining over my shoulders and around my body to catch a glimpse. All their gasps confirm they see what I do—a little girl's hazel eyes that match my own.

M ost of my family left after the bomb about me having a daughter dropped. Everyone but Mom and Hank. Even Fisher made an excuse that he got called into the station to handle something.

Mom slides a cup of tea across the kitchen table to me and stirs a packet of sugar into hers. Not sure why she thinks I want tea right now, so I stand and pull a beer out of the fridge.

"Alcohol isn't going to solve this," she says.

She should be happy I haven't gone for the whiskey bottle yet.

"Tea isn't going to calm me either." I down half the beer.

Hank frowns and I can tell he's unsure where he fits here since he's my stepdad. He's always been great at not overstepping. I've witnessed enough of his lectures to his own kids to know that he's probably armed and ready to give me one, but is hesitant because of the step part of his title in my life. My own dad would probably just say get the paternity test, then fight. Hell, he'd probably tell me to give the little girl up.

"I think we need to slow this all down." My mom splays her hands on the table. "Just take this step by step. You'll go to Minnesota, take the paternity test, and we'll go from there."

I look around the kitchen and huff. "I'm not a father."

Hank picks up the picture, inspecting it again, and sighs before placing it back down.

"Maybe you aren't," my mom says. "Like I said, one step at a time."

I nod and finish off my beer.

"Don't get ahead of yourself here, Jed." Hank's restraint against weighing in must be frayed. "We don't know much at this point. You don't remember her, right?"

I shake my head.

"Then who knows? Although…" He looks at the picture again, seeing what everyone else did. "I mean, it could be coincidental that she looks similar to you. Did I ever tell you that Chevelle was born with red hair?"

Mom glances from the corner of her eyes at her husband.

"No one thought she was ours. We'd make jokes about a mix-up at the hospital. What I'm trying to say is kids change over time. Your mom is right. Don't rush into thinking you're a father just yet."

I stare out my back window. The sky hasn't started to turn dark yet and won't for hours yet since we're so far north. "Regardless, I'm heading to Minnesota."

My mom pats my hand. "Let me go with you."

I shake my head, dead set on doing this on my own. "No. You got your mayor thing and everyone else is busy with their jobs. It's tourist season. This is my responsibility."

She squeezes my hand and there's pain in her eyes. She wants to take this off my plate, handle it for me.

"Come on, Marla, let's give him some time to think," Hank says, standing.

I silently thank him with my eyes because I do want to be alone right now.

My mom leans over to hug me. "Call me if you want to talk."

She picks up both teacups and places them in the sink. Hank pats me on the shoulder and they leave out the front door.

I stand and open the fridge to grab another beer, but spotting the bottle of whiskey, I decide that's a helluva better option. Cracking the bottle open, I take a swig and sit at the kitchen table, picking up the picture.

Sip.

My eyes.

Sip.

My lips.

Sip.

My hair color.

Sip.

My straight nose.

Gulp.

I don't need a fucking paternity test. She's almost a replica of me.

Gulp.

Why wouldn't her mother have told me about her?

The back door opens and the picture drops from my grasp, falling to the table.

I take in Molly dressed in running gear and my dick half chubs. She'd be the perfect distraction right now.

Chapter Four

Molly

"Oh, I thought everyone would still be here." I stand with my hand on the doorknob of Jed and Fisher's place.

Cade and Adam used to live here too. It was Mr. Greene's house with his late wife, and he gave it to the boys as soon as they returned from college and started the brewery. Now that Cade is in a house with Presley and Adam and Lucy are back together, just Jed and Fisher live here.

"Everyone left," Jed murmurs before swigging back a gulp of what I can see is whiskey.

"Sorry. I decided to head over here on a run." I wipe the sweat off my forehead, stepping into the house. "Mind if I grab a water?"

"Help yourself." He lazily throws his hand in the direction of the fridge.

"You okay?" I lift my eyebrows before heading to the fridge and opening it.

"Fine."

I've known Jed since his family moved to town. He's always the happy-go-lucky one, but apparently right now he's not.

"Okay then." I crack open a bottle of water, unzipping my sweater to cool down. Sadly, I still live with my mom about two miles away. I thought it would be a great night to go for a run, and if I swung by here, maybe I could kill two birds with one stone.

"Was Lucy here?" I ask, leaning against the counter.

"Yeah, she ran off with the rest of them."

"Ran off? Was there a fire?" I chuckle. I'm surprised the party is over. Usually the Greenes never cut things short.

"In a way." He takes a swig from the whiskey bottle.

"Okay, what gives? Want to fill me in?" I'm done trying to figure out this situation.

He picks up a picture and tosses it to the edge of the table. I step over and pick it up. It's a picture of a gorgeous woman with a little girl. They're staring at the camera with huge smiles outside what appears to be a park.

"Cute. Who are they?" I place it back down on the table.

"I guess I fucked that woman and the little girl is apparently my daughter."

His tone is so matter of fact that it takes a second for the words to make sense in my head. By the time he takes another sip from the bottle, my eyes are wide and my heart rate has sped up.

I pick the picture back up. Sure enough, I see the resemblance to Jed in the little girl. "Are you surprised?"

His laser-focused eyes lock on mine. "What?"

"You're not celibate by a long shot. I mean… Jed." I tilt my head.

He looks insulted. "I use protection."

I sip my water. "I'm sure you do, but I'm also sure there are times when you might've forgotten or trusted a woman when she said she was on the pill."

He can't be this naive. The man has had his fair share of women, and eventually that kind of thing catches up with you. Although I've crushed on this man most of my life, I'm well aware of his reputation.

"I just told you, I use protection. There's never been a time I didn't."

I hold up the picture. "Well, it looks like it failed." I wave the picture in the air before placing it back down.

"I'm going for a paternity test. She's not mine."

I inhale, because he's crazy if he thinks that little girl isn't his. "Sounds like a plan."

I finish off my water bottle. Tipping the water bottle down, I find Jed's gaze on me. On my breasts specifically. Whatever this is right now, I need to stay clear.

"Well, I'm going to get going." I thumb toward the door.

"Why the rush?" His voice falls to his seductive octave. I've witnessed Jed's game in adolescence and now into adulthood. He hasn't changed up his moves very much.

"What are you going to do? Fuck me to forget her?" I nod toward the picture.

His tongue slips out across his bottom lip. "For old times' sake?"

I shake my head. "That was a long time ago, and you know as well as I do that it was a bad idea then and it would be an even worse one now."

Even I'm surprised at how mature I sound.

He slides back his chair and rises from the table, his eyes never straying from mine.

"What are you doing?" I ask as he steps right in front of me.

He towers over me, having to bend his neck to look directly at me. His arms stretch out and he presses his palms on the edge of the table, caging me in.

"Bad idea, Greene," I say, clenching my thighs together in an attempt to not be turned on.

My mind floods with memories of the time we crossed the line with a quick kiss. It was ages ago and Nikki never did find out, but I didn't know then what I do now. Back then, he was just the hot new guy in school.

"You know as well as I do that we'd rock that bed," he says softly, inching closer. Although I smell the whiskey on his breath, I also smell the cologne on his skin and it's intoxicating.

"You mean I'd rock the bed." I smile and chuckle, but there's nothing on his lips.

"Remember that time you walked in on me at the brewery?" he asks.

"Yes." I swallow hard because that vision has been seared into my memory ever since.

"You ever wonder what could've happened if you'd have come in and locked the door?"

"Listen." I place my hands on his muscled shoulders and nudge him to try to gain some space to think, but he doesn't move. "That might be a wet dream for you, but not for me."

The right side of his lips tips up. He knows I'm lying. This man has filled my dreams for what seems like forever. "I'm not going to touch you until you tell me to."

I draw back. "But you'll lock me to the table?" I quirk an eyebrow.

"It's thrown me, you know. Like someone stuck me in a rocket and flew me to another planet. I mean, me? A dad? What a joke."

My tense shoulders relax at his confession. Jed's not one to show a vulnerable side, but I hear it in his tone. "What exactly are you asking of me?"

I get lost in the golden specks of his green-brown eyes. But he doesn't have to answer for me to know what he wants. It's the same thing most guys come to me for. To lose themselves in me. To escape reality. I know that's what Jed wants right now. The question is, can I be his distraction without being hurt in the end?

He inhales and his gaze skates across my body with fire in his eyes. I won't and can't deny it's a nice feeling to be wanted by Jed Greene.

"We could have some fun." He shrugs. "I'm not sure why we've never fully crossed that line."

"Nikki," I say curtly. "She's the reason."

He breaks the last of the distance between us. Close enough to unnerve me, but still not laying a finger on me. "She doesn't have to know."

Point taken. She's so engrossed in her own world with a new marriage and a baby on the way that her investigative gossip skills have been fuzzy at best.

"Jed." I shake my head. "I'm not who you think I am."

His eyebrows crinkle. "Are you an alien sent here to earth to find our weaknesses?"

I chuckle and roll my eyes. "You know what I mean."

"I'm not sure I do." He steps back and removes his hands from beside my hips, locking them over his chest. It makes his biceps bulge and stretches the ink on some of his tattoos.

"My reputation. I don't do that anymore. In fact, it's been a while since I did." I shake my head, hating that I have to even engage in this conversation. But if Jed thinks I'm the easy lay he can treat however he wants, he's wrong.

He laughs. "Are you serious? You think that's why I'm coming on to you right now? Because some asshole in high school said you sucked his dick?" He grabs the bottle of whiskey, and I'm filled with surprise when he grabs the cap and secures it to the bottle instead of drinking out of it.

"I'm just suggesting that you might think you can use me."

"Looking for a husband, are you?"

"No." I practically stomp my foot.

"You're way overthinking this." He opens the fridge and grabs a bottle of water.

"No, I'm not. I'd say I'm the only one thinking straight right now."

He motions between us. "I thought we were two single, consenting adults who could fuck for a night and move on with our lives. That's all I was thinking. It didn't have anything to do with me thinking you spread your legs for every fucking guy who asks you to."

I zip up my sweatshirt, ready to leave. I have no clue how this ended up getting so out of hand, but I'd best leave him to deal with his shit. "I'm gonna go."

"Fine!"

"Why are you yelling?"

"I'm not yelling!"

"You are."

He lowers his head and pinches the bridge of his nose, inhaling deeply as though I'm the aggravating one. Usually our relationship is full of fun, flirty banter. "I just…" He shakes his head. "Nothing. I'll see you tomorrow at work."

I walk to the back door and twist the knob in my hand, opening it a crack. "See you."

When I step outside, the door shuts, and I freeze when I see a moose standing fifty feet from me. My back hits the door with a thud and my hand fiddles behind my back, trying to find the doorknob without being too noisy or moving too much. Most tourists are afraid of the bears in the area, but us Alaskans know that more of us are hurt by moose than bear in any given year.

The door springs open and I fall back, losing my footing and ending up with my ass on the kitchen floor.

"What the hell?" Jed stands over me. "I thought you

were leaving, but now you're scratching at my door like a cat in heat?"

I point without saying anything. Sure, I've seen moose before, but never one that close.

He follows my finger and shuts the door, flicking the lock. "Shit."

I get up to my feet, brushing off my ass. "I'm here until that thing leaves or you drive me home."

"I know my brother's the sheriff and all, but I'm not cool with drinking and driving."

We both look at the half-empty bottle of whiskey on the table.

"Then I guess you have a houseguest for a little while." I open the fridge, grab a beer, and head into the family room. "Unless you want to scare it away."

"I doubt it's as easily scared as you are," he says.

"Excuse me?" I spin around to face him.

"You heard me, don't act like you didn't."

"When did we go back to the fourth grade?"

"When you typecast me as wanting to get my hands in your panties because of some rumor some dipshit started in high school."

"It's legit, okay!" I scream, beyond annoyed. That incident damaged me in a way I never fully recovered from.

"Well, sue me if I wanted to fuck you because you're hot and you came into my house half-clothed and covered in sweat with your tits hanging out. You flirt with me all the damn time. I know you want me as badly as I want you."

I open my mouth but say nothing because I can't refute what he's saying. "I just..."

His arm wraps around my stomach and his mouth lands on the hollow of my ear. "Just what?"

His breath on my neck sends a swarm of goose bumps down my arms. The heat from his body seeps into mine and it feels so good I can't bring myself to push him away. "No strings, no commitment, no relationship."

I close my eyes, knowing he'll agree. I'm the stupid ass who is secretly hoping this isn't my demise. I don't want a relationship. Marriage isn't for me. And I do want to stop wanting Jed Greene. Maybe I'll be lucky and he's a shitty lay.

"Deal," he says softly, his lips gently moving against my neck when he speaks. "So I have permission to touch you?"

I shake my head and suck in a breath. "Just fuck me, Jed."

"With fervor." He bends and moves his shoulder into my stomach, carrying me upstairs fireman style.

Yeah, I knew it was unlikely he'd be a shitty lay.

Chapter Five

Molly

Jed opens up his bedroom door and lays me on the bed, then takes the beer still in my hand and places it on his nightstand. My hands move to the top of my leggings, expecting this will be a quickie and then I'll go home, but he stays standing between my dangling legs.

His eyes are fierce and filled with lust. There's no possible way he's wanted this as much as I have all these years. Sure, we've toed that line of flirtatious touches and sexual innuendos, but that's just how we've always been. Everyone knows Jed goes after what he wants, never accepting the word no, pushing and pushing until it's a yes.

I sit up to rest my weight on my elbows, wondering if this isn't going to go where I assumed. Our eyes lock and his tongue slides out of his mouth, wetting his bottom lip.

"Are you sure?" he asks.

Although now I'm wondering if he's having doubts, I nod anyway, ignoring the small tug-of-war still being fought inside me. I rarely take anything for myself. It's taken me over ten years to get this close to graduating with my master's in speech pathology because I had to work to pay for those classes, plus help my mom. But I've wanted

Jed Greene for a long time, and tonight, I'm going to take it. I'm going to take it and enjoy it and move on.

His knee presses to my inner knee and he widens my legs, then bends forward until my back hits the mattress as he hovers over me. I inhale, taking in his masculine scent and gaining the courage to do this. To take what I want and not think about anyone else.

He grabs a hold of his shirt from the back and pulls it off his body, exposing his six-pack abs and light trail of hair dipping down past his jeans. My fingers itch to travel down his chest, to lick every indent and rest my head there and inhale his citrus and cedar scent.

He's going to break me, make me feel things if he takes his time. I need us to quench this thirst, be in the moment, then move on. So I push him back and rise to kneel on the bed, placing my hands on his shoulders and dipping my lips to his chest. He pulls out my ponytail holder and my dark hair falls over my shoulders. Then he threads his fingers through the strands as I explore his body, my fingers fiddling with the button of his jeans.

His stomach indents when he sucks in a breath after his pants open and I slide down the zipper.

"Damn, you feel good," he whispers.

"You've barely touched me," I murmur with humor in my tone. I take a break from pulling down his jeans to unzip and pull my sweatshirt off my body, leaving me in a sports bra and leggings.

"I meant your hands on me." He pushes his jeans down and they flop to the floor.

When he steps out of them, I draw back and take in the sight of him in only a pair of olive-green boxer briefs. He's ripped, which I figured from the time he spends at the gym. Not that he's a gym rat, but he goes religiously, either before or after work. The deep-set V on his lower abdomen is exactly like I imagined.

For a moment, our eyes fix on one another's and I swallow past the dryness in my throat. Needing to stop these weird moments like we're getting lost in one another, my hands reach for the bottom of my sports bra.

Jed touches my forearms to stop me. "Allow me."

"Aren't you a gentleman," I say and lower my arms to my sides.

He kneels with one knee on the bed, leaning forward, and his fingers slide under the fabric of my sports bra, my skin prickling from his touch. The tightness of the elastic releases from my body and he tugs it over my breasts, which pop out one by one, until he pulls the fabric over my head and tosses it to the side of the bed.

I've never felt this vulnerable with a man. That's a lie. I did once—with this exact man—and I don't want to ever feel that again, so I press my body to his, wrapping my arms around his neck and tackling him so he has no choice but to lie on top of me on the bed. I want his body to bury mine.

"Whoa," he says, but chuckles lightly, his fingers grazing down the side of my breast toward my leggings.

His fingers dip between my thighs, and since the fabric is thin, I clench when I feel his touch travel up and down my core. A moan escapes me and his mouth dips to mine, his tongue sliding into my mouth without waiting for approval. It doesn't surprise me. Jed isn't really an "ask permission" kind of guy once he knows he's got it. Besides, I'm the one who tackled him to the bed, so it's clear I'm a willing participant.

Explosions go off when he strokes me and I taste the whiskey on his tongue. I grip his shoulders. Our kiss is intoxicating. Of course, Jed kisses as well as he does everything else in his life. When he tears his lips off mine, closing the kiss, I grumble from the loss of his warmth.

He trails his lips down my neck and between the valley of my breasts while he hooks his fingers into the sides of my leggings, tugging them down my body. The job is harder than he expected, so his mouth pops off my breast and he sits up to use all his strength to strip me.

"Jesus," he whispers. "Next time, how about a skirt?"

I'm finally free of the tight fabric and my stomach sprouts with a seed of hope that there will be a next time.

How pathetic am I? I already told myself this is a one and done.

"A little hard work won't kill you." I place my hand on his hardening dick that's straining the front of his boxer briefs.

"I shouldn't sweat from unclothing you," he says and leans forward, allowing me better access to him.

I squeeze his dick through the thin fabric, remembering that day I walked in on him. He's crazy to think I didn't feel the pull between us in that moment, and although I entertained doing something at the moment, I was glad I didn't.

Then again, here I am now.

"Stop thinking so much and just enjoy this." His mouth dips to my neck.

As my back sinks down into the mattress once more and my hand moves away from his hardening cock, I close my eyes at the feeling of the weight of his body over mine. Raising my arm above my head, he links our fingers and grinds himself into my center. A moan slips free, and I raise my hips off the mattress to try to chase that pleasure once again. His free hand cups my breast and his thumb strokes my nipple, sending more sensations down to my core.

"More. I need more," I beg.

Jed laughs into my skin. "Then strip me down."

He raises his hips, stripping me of the pleasure our dry humping was providing, so I hurriedly tug the boxers down his legs. He helps me, using his feet to get them off completely.

"Condom?" I ask before things move too far along.

He smiles at me. Reaching over, he pulls one out of his nightstand drawer and rips it open.

As I wait for him to roll it down his length, I stare at the ceiling as though I'm some virgin and it's my first time. My heartbeat is so out of control it *feels* like it's my first time with a guy. Before I can mentally tally the repercussions if knowledge of this gets out of this room, the tip of his dick is pushing at my entrance and his hungry eyes are focused on mine.

"Hey there," he says, knowing my mind is far away from this moment. "You sure about this?"

He inches himself in and I widen my legs, nodding quickly. "Yes."

I groan when he continues to sink into me until he's fully inside. God, he feels just as I thought he would.

He draws out and slides back in, sinking through my wetness. Every nerve ending in my body feels as if it's on fire and screaming for more.

Our lips collide, and soon we're both grasping one another as though we can't get close enough. He whispers praises of how good I feel, how much he thought about being inside me, and all of his words make the ache for him that much deeper.

This man knows exactly what he's doing. Shifting my one leg up on his shoulder, he drives into me, his gaze darkened with arousal as he stares at my bare breasts bouncing with each thrust.

"Harder. Faster."

A wicked smile creases his lips. "I knew you were just as insatiable as me."

I shake my head, a comeback somewhere far off in the distance. "Just fuck me."

As though he'd been waiting for the magic words, he drives into me with more force than before. Over and over, he thrusts inside me as though he's exorcising his own demons while he's fucking me. My orgasm builds and builds. I clench to keep it at bay, wanting to wring every moment of enjoyment out of this while I can.

He's watching me with an intensity I've not seen from him before, and when he places the pad of his thumb on my clit and softly circles it, I almost combust. Every muscle in my body is strung tight as a bow, ready to snap. But he only applies enough pressure so I know he's there, not enough to unravel me.

My back arches, begging for something, anything, and he licks his lips, staring at the offering of my tits. I wish he had five hands so he could caress me everywhere. Sweat pools between my breasts and I watch as one drop of sweat falls down his chest onto me. More curses leave his mouth and he fucks me with the fervor he promised until my body shudders under him and I gasp, spewing nonsensical words of praise for him.

Lowering my leg, he sucks on my tit, moving in and out of me in a rhythm that makes him growl and groan until he stills. His mouth comes off my breast with a pop and he groans, though it sounds more like a growl, and he comes.

After he collapses on me for a moment, he slips out of me and rolls to my side. Both of us are left gasping, staring at the ceiling.

I knew he'd be good, but did he really have to be the best I've ever had? This is a cruel joke.

"I'll be right back," he says, rising off the bed. I watch his perfect naked ass go to his bedroom door.

Lost for only a moment, the shutting of the bathroom door jars me back to reality. I just slept with Nikki's brother. I just slept with my boss.

I sit up and grab my clothes, quickly pulling up my leggings. My arms get tangled in my sports bra and my head goes into the armhole. "Fuck."

"Well, this is a switch. A woman running out on me," Jed says from somewhere behind me.

"Just help me with this," I say, trying to free myself of the damn bra, only to get more entwined.

"I don't know, I could have my way with you like this." He flicks my nipple with his finger. "Are you into BDSM?"

"Jed!" I yell.

His hands mold to my hips and he bends down, his tongue circling my nipple. "That feel better?"

My body betrays me, and I arch my back, offering him more.

"Greedy girl," he says and continues to suck on my tits.

All the muscles in my core pull tight again. He's right. I am greedy when it comes to him.

He raises his head and pulls the fabric off my body. "Stay."

I meet his gaze. "Okay," I say, knowing it's a stupid decision. But if I don't leave, then this counts as only doing this once, right?

Orgasms like the one Jed gave me have a tendency to blur reality.

Jed

*L*eaving Molly in my bed the next morning, I shut my bedroom door and head downstairs to make coffee.

Fisher's in his sheriff uniform, bent over, head in the fridge. I spot the discarded picture from last night on the kitchen table and turn away. That's a reality I'm not ready for just yet.

"Who's your visitor?" he asks, taking three eggs over to the stove where a pan with butter sizzles.

"What?" I grab my coffee mug and pour myself a cup. The one good thing about living with Fisher is that the coffee is always prepared as long as he's up and at home.

"The moans, the banging. I thought you two were going to end up in my bedroom."

I sip my coffee, giving myself a minute to think. Molly and I did get a little crazy last night. I knew she'd be great in bed, but damn, she's any guy's dream girl. The thought of her learning any of those moves from other guys sours the taste in my mouth. But I quickly shake off the feeling of jealousy.

"Sorry about that."

He chuckles.

Fisher and I have secrets. There are things we're willing

to keep between us, so I could tell him it's Molly and he wouldn't say a word, but she was adamant that no one in the family knows.

"You don't have to apologize. I'm just curious who you got over here so fast. I was gone two hours tops." He cracks the eggs and drops them in the pan.

"Are you questioning my game?" I laugh, hoping to keep veering this conversation away from who the girl might be. Fisher should be leaving once he eats, then Molly can leave and no one will be the wiser. The problem is that I wouldn't mind one for the road before she goes, especially since the picture sitting on the table is causing the same tightening feeling in my chest as it did last night.

"Nah, I know you got game. Although you're not as good as me." He places the eggs on a plate and grabs the toast waiting in the toaster before sitting at the table. Picking up the picture, he looks at it while forking his eggs. "What are you going to do?"

I sit next to him and sigh. "Book a flight to Minnesota. I have to find out if she's mine."

"You still don't remember the mom?" He buries his head in his plate.

I'm glad he can't see my face. I'm fully aware I'm handling this like a douche, but I can't get a handle on it. "No."

"Maybe there's a letter or something with the will."

I nod. "I hope so."

The noise of a car engine revving up our driveway rings through the house and we both lock eyes.

"Mom," I say.

"Marla," he says at the same time.

I blow out a breath. "She's not gonna let this go."

His forehead crinkles. "And she should? You have a daughter whether you like it or not." Fisher quickly finishes off his eggs and takes his plate to the sink. He drops it in, turns on the tap for a moment to rinse his dish, then shuts it off. "I'm out. See you tonight."

"I'll be at the brewery late," I say, refilling my cup of coffee.

"You better hope your girl stays upstairs." He laughs and grabs his keys as my mom opens the back door. "Good morning, Marla." He kisses her on the cheek and walks out.

"'Morning, Fisher. There's an accident on Whitespring Road, by the bridge."

He smiles and tips his head. "Thanks for the heads-up."

"What would Fisher do without you?" I joke, but my mom doesn't smile. She actually scowls. For a moment, I wonder if she knows who's upstairs in my bed.

"What would *you* do without *me*?" She goes to the sink and rinses off Fisher's plate again before putting it in the dishwasher.

"That's not mine."

She rolls her eyes. The back door opens again and Rylan walks in.

"We're gonna be late for school," he says.

"You have plenty of time." Mom continues to load the dishwasher with the other dishes in the sink and Rylan flops down at a seat at the table.

"It's fine really, I got this," I say, trying to take the sponge out of her hands, but she doesn't budge.

"Ry, wait for me outside."

His head falls back and he groans. I'm with him. We both know she's about to tell me how it is.

Once the door shuts behind him, she turns off the water and tosses the sponge in the sink. "I understand it's a shock, but buck up, Jed, and deal with your responsibilities."

"Buck up?" I bite down my laugh.

She crosses her arms and juts out her hip, her eyes laser focused on mine. "You find this funny? That there's a little girl who might be yours out in the world? Whose mother has died and now she's all alone? You should've been on a flight this morning."

Her words sober my mood. I still can't wrap my head around it. Less than twenty-four hours ago, my life was how it'd always been, and now everything has changed. Everything. It's gonna take me a hot minute to get used to the idea of being a father, let alone start acting like one.

"I just found out last night." I sit at the table, spotting Molly lingering in the doorway with wide eyes. I shake for her to make herself scarce.

"Exactly, and you should've booked a flight last night so you could be on that plane this morning. What are you doing right now?" She waves her hand down my body.

Since I'm in track pants and nothing else, I shrug. "I—"

"What? You're sitting around here, drinking." She walks over to the table and swings the bottom of the whiskey bottle like a pendulum in front of me. "Alcohol solves this how?"

"I'm not sure what you expect from me? This is a complete shock. I don't remember the mom and I feel bad for the little girl, but she's probably not mine."

"Not yours?" Her voice would scare away the moose from last night if it were still there. "Have you seen the picture? She's practically a carbon copy of you!"

"I gotta clear up some stuff at the bar." The excuse sounds lame even to my ears.

"No, you don't." She shakes her head. "You need to get

your ass down to Minnesota and take that test. Meet the little girl." She digs into her purse and slams a piece of paper on the table. It takes me a second to realize it's a print-out for a plane ticket. "You leave this evening. I was gracious enough to give you time to talk with Cade."

Again, I spot Molly from the corner of my eye, this time with her shoes in her hand.

"But you better make that flight, and you better get your head out of your ass. Man up, Jed." She swings her purse over her shoulder and stalks toward the door. "And go through your mail. Seriously, you two." She shakes her head and leaves.

The back door slams and I hear her yell at Rylan to stop playing basketball and get in the car.

Sorry, little guy.

Molly walks into the room and sits at the table, pulling on her shoes. "Guess I'll see you later. I'm sure Cade and I can handle the bar."

I watch her, and all I can think of is how I want one more for the road. Escaping into this woman is exactly what I need right now. "Do you have to go so soon?"

She finishes tying her shoes and stands, putting on her sweatshirt. "I do."

I swing my arm around her waist and pull her toward me, grabbing ahold of her zipper and tugging it down.

"Get that mischievous smirk off your lips. I'm going home. We talked about this."

She wiggles in my arms, and I cast small kisses to her stomach. "Just one more time."

"That's what you said last night. Twice."

She doesn't fight me, and I know it's because she wants me too. Hell, I've never been so compatible with someone in bed.

"I have to find Lucy so I have some hope of graduating." She pushes at my shoulders.

I don't know what she means by that, and right now, I don't care. "Come on," I say, my hands inching along her back and running up to the hem of her sports bra. "You know you want to stay."

"Where's Fisher?" she asks, her voice a little breathy.

"Gone."

"And any other Greenes coming today?"

I shake my head on her stomach.

She widens her legs and sits down to straddle me on the chair. Taking her action as a yes, I push the sweatshirt off her shoulders and it falls to the floor.

"Good decision." I pull her mouth down to mine, sliding my tongue into her mouth.

Damn, she's amazing. I'm not sure if it's because this allows me to forget what's on my plate at the moment or if it's just her, but I don't want to stop. Her hand is on my dick, which has no problem saluting the occasion, when we hear another vehicle pull up the driveway.

"Fuck," I say, and she hops off me, trying to get her bra repositioned. She runs to the back door, but we already hear a voice coming that way. Since when does everyone use the back door? "Go back upstairs."

Her shoulders sag. "I have things to do."

I pull her toward me with my hand on her hip. "*We* have things to do. I'll get rid of whoever it is."

She runs to the stairs as the back door opens and Cade emerges on his cell phone. "As long as it's what you want."

Wedding talk again. I roll my eyes, trying to get my dick to cooperate and deflate so Cade's none the wiser.

"I'll tell him. Okay, I'm here now. Love you too."

He hangs up and I stare blankly at him. I'm annoyed

that he's here, no doubt on either Hank or my mom's suggestion.

"My mom has already been here this morning. You can go."

Since this was his house first and he lived here forever, he takes a cup from the cabinet and fills it with coffee before sitting at the table, glancing at the picture. Everyone looks at that damn picture.

"I hear you're leaving tonight. No worries, I'll handle the bar. I'm sure Molly will take a few extra shifts." He sips his coffee and waits.

I roll my eyes and spot Molly's sweatshirt on the floor. I kick it under the table, away from Cade.

"I'll be back tomorrow," I say.

He pauses, but he looks at me over the rim of the cup. "So that's how you're playing this? You're going to pretend it's nothing?"

Cade probably knows me the best out of all the siblings in our family.

"You can't do that, Jed. She's more than likely yours."

"I don't even remember her mother," I say.

He shrugs. "Doesn't mean it isn't true. Maybe you'll find out more answers in Minnesota. Like where you two met."

"Maybe, but why would a woman I don't even remember put me in the will and on the birth certificate? I don't know the woman, but she knew my first and last name? She didn't even want to tell me about the child when she was alive, but in death, she leaves me as her sole caregiver?"

He sighs. Cade's a shit ton more responsible than me. Hence why he's already engaged, owns a house with his fiancée, and is probably not far off from becoming a dad himself.

"Just go and get some answers. The quicker you do it, the sooner you know if she's yours—which, for the record, I don't have any doubts that she is." He looks at the picture one more time before standing. "I've got things handled here."

"I have an appointment—"

"I know, and I'll take care of it."

I groan because we both know I'm the better salesperson. I schmooze the potential clients, while Cade is all facts and spreadsheets. "He's really—"

"Stop it. I know Nate from Lucky's."

We both know Nate from Lucky's bar in the neighboring town of Lake Starlight, but he's been reluctant to put our beers in his bar. My assumption is because if people like them, he's afraid they might drive out to us instead of going to his bar. But he has a regular following there. This is a huge opportunity for us, and I hate to be the one who isn't going to close the deal.

"Fine. This couldn't come at a worse time." I push the heels of my hands into my eye sockets.

Cade dumps his coffee and puts the cup in the dishwasher. Presley has trained him well. "Listen, I know you're scared. It's okay to be scared."

I say nothing. Cade knows me about as well as my mother, which is why both of them came to me this morning.

"But you're a great person. You aren't your father. If she's yours, it'll all work out. And you have all of us here to help you." He pats me on the back.

I nod and stare at the floor. Cade follows my vision and bends down to pick up Molly's sweatshirt. He lifts it with a devilish glint in his eyes.

My stomach drops.

"Burying yourself in pussy isn't going to change the

fact that you probably have a daughter." He hands me the sweatshirt.

He must not know it's Molly's, otherwise he'd be starting in on lecture number two for the day. The guy needs his own TED talk.

I take it, thankful Cade isn't very perceptive about our employee's attire. "Thanks, Cade. I'll call you when I know something."

He walks toward the back door. "Good luck, man."

The door shuts, and half a minute later, Molly barrels into the room. She snags the sweatshirt from my hands and looks out the kitchen window, waiting for Cade to disappear.

"It's been real," she says and flees out the door before I can remind her we weren't finished.

Chapter Seven

"Until later."

-Jed

Molly

I'm walking down Jed's driveway, shaking my head that I actually slept with him and more than once. My body breaks out in shivers when I remember how skillful his hands and lips were. The man knows how to please a woman. Of course he does though. He's had a long line of women.

The honk of a horn surprises me and I jolt back, finding Nikki waving ecstatically from her Jeep. She stops at the end of his driveway and I silently curse myself for not running down the driveway to the street rather than walking. At least then I could've said I was just out for a jog.

It takes her longer than usual to get out of her car. She's only five months, but talking to her, you'd think she was ready to pop. Although she does seem kind of big.

"What are you doing here?" She walks past the front of her Jeep and gives me a hug.

"Nothing, just cutting through by the lake." I never go toward the lake since that's where the accident happened with Laurie Greene, Hank's first wife.

But the mention of the lake does the trick, making Nikki's mind go to the accident that changed everyone's life and not why I'm leaving her brothers' house in the morning.

"Did you hear?" She glances back at the house. "Jed is a dad. Had a one-night stand and now finds out he's got a three-year-old. I guess the mom passed away and has no other relatives."

I open my mouth as if I'm shocked—even though I allowed him to use me last night as a distraction from dealing with his problems. "Really? That's crazy."

"I mean, we all knew eventually it might happen. The man can't keep it in his pants, you know?"

I nod.

She smacks my shoulder. "What is wrong with you? My brother, the most irresponsible man we know, is going to be a father. And your reaction is to nod?"

I shrug. "I guess I'm just shocked."

She studies me for a minute, making me uneasy. "He has to go to Minnesota. I came here to push him toward making the right decision. You know how he is when he feels cornered."

I nod. I do. He'll look for any escape and I made myself an easy one last night.

"Are you sure you're okay?" She's clearly picking up that something isn't right.

I smack on a smile. "I'm good. Just surprised, and I didn't get much sleep last night." Another lie, so I cross my fingers behind my back, feeling horrible for being untruthful with my best friend.

"But you decided on a run?"

"Was hoping it would clear my mind. There's something going on with my clinical. The family of the boy I was working with is moving back to the reservation, which leaves me with no full clinical case to present."

Her shoulders sag. "Oh, Mol." She runs her hand down my arm. "I'm sorry."

The last thing I want is her pity. "It's fine. I just have to find a new child to help. I'm going to talk to Lucy today."

Her eyes light up. "That's a great idea. I'm sure she'll know of someone."

"I hope so."

"Want to go up and surprise Jed with me?"

I look back at the house I just ran away from. "Nah. I think that's a brother and sister moment."

"He'll probably kick me out."

"Doubt it. I'm sure he could use some guidance right now." Which is the truth. The man is going to blow this if he doesn't get his head on straight.

"It was good seeing you. We really need a girls' night out." She hugs me.

I cling to her a little harder, the guilt building inside me for deceiving her. Nikki was clear years ago that she didn't want me to cross that line with any of her brothers and I swore to her I never would.

"Definitely. Call me." I squeeze her one more time and release her.

"Are you sure you're okay?"

I nod, walking away. "It's just this school stuff. I cannot delay this graduation. It's taken me forever."

She watches me go. "It will all work out. I know it will."

I smile and jog in place. "Go do what you do best. Tell your brother what he needs to do."

She salutes me. We both laugh and I jog away until I'm out of sight. As my footfalls slow to a walking pace, my mind takes me back to the memory of the first time I saw Jed Greene.

"Did you see all the new Greene kids?" Melanie asked me in the hallway after science class.

"Some of them." All I'd heard was that some of the Greenes' cousins were going to start attending our school. Apparently there was a quarterback who was going to give Cade Greene a run for the position.

"Well, wait until you see Jed Greene." She put her hand over her heart and sighed. Melanie had a flair for the dramatics.

"Senior?" I asked.

"Yes, and you know how everyone drools over the other Greene guys?"

I nodded, stopping at my locker. Cade Greene had been with Reese forever, so he'd been off the market. Fisher wasn't really the type to settle down, and Xavier was always with Clara more than he was with the football team. All three of them were so different, but they were all hot as hell. Just unavailable for different reasons. "Let me guess, this Jed guy is hotter?"

Her back hit the locker and she nodded. "So hot. He's got these dimples and he's so tall and so muscular. His ass…" She moaned.

I laughed and shook my head, grabbing my calculator for math homework I needed to finish in study hall. "You are so boy obsessed."

Melanie was. I hadn't hit that stage yet and I wondered when I would ever have a real crush on a guy. While most of my friends talked about boys constantly and wanted to play games like spin the bottle, I was meh at best about them. Maybe because my dad had run out on us and I'd seen the repercussions of a woman being left with a broken heart.

"I guess I'll find out when I see him."

"You'll know when you do."

I shut my locker and we continued to walk down the hall. Melanie had English and never really cared about getting into trouble, so she usually walked me to study hall then sauntered into English. She had Mr. Henderson wrapped around her finger.

"*See you,*" I said and turned into the classroom where study hall was held.

I stopped in the doorway because there was a big body at the desk I usually used, a circle of guys surrounding him. They were all seniors, football players, so I ducked my head and beelined to the back of the room, taking a seat.

"Hey, Monroe, I'm sure Jed won't mind if you sit on his lap," that asshole Matty said, making Jed turn around.

My cheeks heated and anger burned in my belly.

Jed half stood from the desk. "Am I in your seat?"

I shook my head, never truly making eye contact. "No. There aren't assigned seats here."

"My mom didn't raise an asshole. Here." He stood.

I glanced at him and my eyes locked with his. Holy shit. Melanie was right. His eyes were stunning. For a moment, I couldn't find my voice. "It's fine."

"Hey, Jed, Monroe doesn't mind sitting on laps. Although she much prefers kneeling." Matty laughed and so did a few other people around him.

I rolled my eyes. "Keep telling lies," I murmured to myself.

The one time I agreed to go to a party with Melanie this summer, Matty was there and wanted to play seven minutes in heaven. When we got out, he pretended he was zipping up his jeans. The next day, Melanie called to tell me that he was telling everyone I sucked him off in the closet.

"Really, take your seat," Jed's deep voice said.

My gaze flickered up and up until I was staring at Jed Greene. He had his books in hand and was waiting for me to get out of my seat.

"Everyone, sit down and start working. There's no talking, no phones, no note passing." Mrs. DeLuca walked in.

Everyone scrambled to a seat. Not having a choice, I murmured a thank you and beelined to my usual desk. I buried myself in my *math work, unable to really concentrate on it because all I could think about was Jed.*

When study hall ended, I gathered my books.

Jed stood at the end of the aisle, a charismatic smile on his lips. "Mind showing me where my next class is?"

We walked out of the classroom side by side.

I swallowed down the dryness that coated my throat. "Where do you have to go?"

"I knew you were a smart man, Greene." Matty patted him on the back, but Jed shoved Matty into the row of lockers outside the classroom.

"I hate assholes who spread rumors," Jed said.

My entire body lit up. I finally understood Melanie's boy craziness.

Jed pulled out his schedule to show me.

"I'm right next door to your classroom. We have to go upstairs," I said.

"Show me the way." He waved his arm out in front of him.

The two of us walked down the hall, then up the stairs to the upper classrooms. He lingered, waving to a few people, and I wondered how a guy could be so popular in only his first week at school. Sunrise Bay was small and could be cliquey, but they'd opened their arms wide for this guy. That made me like him even more.

The rest of the week, he asked to walk me to my next class. We lingered in the hallway until the last bell, talking about nothing and everything.

On Friday afternoon, he rested his arm above the lockers, hovering over me.

"You go to football games?" he asked. His body, being so close to mine, sent a thrill through me.

"Everyone goes to the football games. There isn't a ton to do in this town."

He bit down on his bottom lip and stared at me. "I have this weird superstition—and feel free to say no—but I always play better if I kiss a girl before the game. I wondered if…"

"Sure," I agreed. The idea of kissing Jed was too appealing to turn down. "We could meet behind the concession stand?"

Afterward, I kicked myself for sounding like a pro at the whole making out thing. I'd never been behind the concession stand with a boy.

"Perfect. I'll meet you there once I'm suited up." His grin was wide. The bell rang and he leaned down, his lips at my ear. "Until later."

The loud honking of a horn behind me pulls me out of my memory. Damn it.

"Girl, you're still not home?" Nikki pulls alongside me. "Come on, I'm driving you."

I get inside her Jeep, needing the distraction from memory lane.

"So what did Jed say?" I ask.

She rolls her eyes and sighs. "He's reminding me of the douche he was in high school. Remember when he thought our dad was awesome and he had everything laid at his feet? I don't get it though… he grew up when he found out all that shit about my dad."

I don't defend Jed by saying he's not that guy anymore. Even if I fell for the guy he was when he first came to Sunrise Bay, he's not him anymore. Jed's just scared. He's terrified he can't be the dad he wants to be. Just like Nikki had issues with men because of their dad, Jed has the same scars. He thinks he's his father's son, but I know he has this. He just has to believe in himself.

I lay my head on the headrest behind me and sigh. I can't get wrapped up in this situation and convince him he'll be a great dad. Then again, I shouldn't have slept with him last night if that's the case. Jed Greene's always been that untouchable gem glimmering in the distance. I should have kept him there last night, because as Nikki slows at my house, I can't help feeling like I've deceived her. And I swore to her all those years ago that our friendship was more important than any boy, especially her brother.

Jed

People complain about Alaska, but Minnesota isn't all that warm either. I walk into the lawyer's high-rise building downtown, dressed in slacks and a button-down, feeling very much like my fucking father. All I need is a pair of loafers and I'd be him. But I'm pretty sure my usual casual attire of jeans and a T-shirt won't cut it in this circumstance.

Looking at the directory on the side of the wall by the elevator bank, I find David Webb's name and round the corner to press the up button. The office building is pretty busy, but then again, it's first thing in the morning. After flying in last night, I was wiped out from my night with Molly, so I crashed hard.

Taking the elevator up to the sixteenth floor, I step out and follow the signs to David Webb's office and walk in. There's a small waiting room with a receptionist behind a glass partition. She welcomes me with a smile and a roam of her eyes.

"I'm here to see David Webb," I say.

"Yes. You're Jed Greene, correct?" She picks up a file folder.

I wish I could see the contents of the file. I can imagine the notes. "Idiot who doesn't have his shit together."

"Yes, I am."

"Come this way. David is expecting you." She waves for me to follow her.

I head toward the opening to the hallway that his office must be down and realize that the woman is taller than most as she rises out of her chair. She's very mom-looking with long blonde hair and a willowy frame.

Stopping inside the first doorway, she says, "David, Jed is here." She walks in and hands him my folder.

He smiles at me as if we're old buddies and I'm here to catch up, maybe go grab some lunch. Hello, the man showed up at my house—with my entire family there—and pretty much stamped *Womanizer* on my forehead. How the hell do I not know I got someone pregnant? Let alone remember who the hell the woman is? The anger rises inside me again that this woman never tried to tell me I was going to be a father. I'm not a deadbeat, I can take care of my responsibilities—even if the past thirty-six hours doesn't bode well for that argument.

But there's a difference between being told you have a three-year-old and you're now the sole provider for her and being told someone is pregnant and having close to a year to figure shit out. Can I really be blamed that it's taking me a minute to wrap my head around the idea?

"Jed, have a seat. Thank you, Renee." He smiles widely.

As I slide by Renee through the door, I spot a picture of the two of them on the shelf behind him, three kids standing in front of the happy couple. So at least when he said he was a friend of Tanya's, it wasn't code for him fucking her. That would've made things even more uncomfortable right now.

I offer my hand and he shakes it with vigor. Maybe this is a pissing match after all.

"Have a seat. How was your flight?" he asks.

I sit in the leather seat and the door clicks shut behind me, Renee giving us privacy. I'm not sure why though. Pillow talk and all.

"Good."

"Glad to hear that. So…" He takes the file Renee gave him and opens it. "You have an appointment at a medical office this morning." He hands me a paper. "You have to be there within the hour. They already have E—the minor's DNA. I paid the extra for a rush on the results, so we'll know by tomorrow sometime."

I take the piece of paper, glance at the time, and fold it. "And you'll call me?"

"I think it's best that we meet here again. If everything comes out like I think it will, you'll be able to head home the day after with her."

Dryness coats my throat and my heart races. "I'm sorry?"

"Listen, I know this is all a shock to you, but the minor's life has already taken a turn for the worse here. Delaying in getting her where she'll remain permanently is only going to cause her more heartache. She's very confused right now."

That makes two of us.

"Where is she right now?"

He sighs. "She's actually at my house. I was able to pull some strings to keep her out of foster care."

"There's really no one else? Not one family member?" Coming from a family as big as mine, I cannot imagine not having one biological relative to call on. Hell, if something happened to Mom and Hank, we'd all be pitching in to take care of Rylan.

David shakes his head, his semi-smile diminishing. I wonder how close he and Tanya were. "Not that she ever spoke of, and you're mentioned in the will. Tanya was a private person."

"Have you tried to find someone now that she's passed?"

His eyes narrow, and I'm ashamed that what he's thinking about me is true. Leaning back in his chair, he studies me. "Is there something you want to say, Jed?"

I shake my head. "Nothing until after the paternity test."

"I'd rather just talk now."

"There's nothing to talk about until we know that I'm her father."

He sighs and looks out his window for a moment before his gaze lands on me again. He's got that dad look down pat. I feel like I'm being scorned by Hank.

"Em—the minor…" He pauses for an uncomfortably long time. "Oh, screw it. Your daughter's name is Emilia, and she's three years old and having nightmares. She's confused and doesn't hardly talk to anyone but my six-year-old daughter. Tanya, her mother, was her life. They didn't have any other family because, from what I assume based on the little amount Tanya ever spoke to Renee about it, she more or less abandoned her family after high school. Apparently it wasn't a good situation and obviously isn't one she wanted to put her daughter in."

Emilia, I say over and over in my head. Emilia Greene has a nice ring to it.

"So if you're going to find out what everyone pretty much knows already—that you are in fact her father—just to try to find someone else to take responsibility for her, I'd rather get papers for you to sign over your rights ready now."

My forehead creases and I scowl, standing from my chair. "I'm not going to sign over my rights."

"Then why are you asking about other family members?" He stands and places his hands on his hips.

"Because I'm a single guy. I thought maybe there are better options for her out there. Which is why I wanted to have this conversation *after* the results came back. And maybe everyone's so sure she's mine because she looks like me, but she's only three years old. Who's to say that Tanya didn't have a type and there's some guy who looks just like me out there somewhere who actually is the dad? I still don't remember her. And although everyone thinks I'm some womanizing manwhore, I'm actually not. I get names and remember faces."

I walk away from the desk, staring out the window at the streets of Minneapolis. She's out there somewhere. Emilia, the little girl who might be my daughter.

"You met her on vacation. She was working as a waitress at a hotel bar at a resort on the ocean," Renee says. I turn to find her in the doorway. She shrugs. "Sorry, thin doors."

"Vacation?"

"You were with a group of guys, someone who had a lot of money and was showing it off with big tips and buying rounds." She steps inside the office. "You'd been flirting with her the entire trip, and the last night, you begged her to stick around after her shift. She reluctantly did, and you both got drunk and went back to your room. You woke up alone because she left after you passed out."

I shove my hands in my pockets, pissed off that this woman knows the story and I have no recollection.

"Fuck," I say, slowly piecing it together. Fisher, Cam, and I were there for a bachelor party. I run my hand through my hair, wishing I hadn't left the picture back at the hotel room. "Why didn't she ever reach out?"

"She felt as though it was what it was, a one-night

stand. She worried about you wanting to take Emilia away."

I scowl. "She didn't even know me."

Renee nods. "That's true. She did an amazing job with her though. Emilia's struggling right now, and when you meet her, she probably won't say much, because she's shy. But she's so smart and sweet. She loves animals."

I put up my hand. "If she's mine, you don't have to sell her to me. I'll talk to you two after the test results."

"Jed? If—"

I put up my hand to stop David's line of thinking. "I'll be here with two plane tickets."

Sure, I might not know what the hell I'm doing, but I'm not going to abandon my own daughter.

I walk out the door and onto the elevator, then back onto the streets of Minneapolis, unsure what the hell I'm gonna do. Now that I do remember Tanya, the probability of me being Emilia's father is pretty damn good if my math is correct.

That night, after I've been poked and swabbed, I walk the streets until most of the stores are closed, leaving only the restaurants and bars open. I'm not in the mood to be around a lot of people, so I head to my hotel, my phone burning a hole in my pocket. I want to call Cam or Fisher and ask them if they remember her. But what's it going to do? I remember Tanya and I've been so hell-bent on believing the little girl isn't mine because I didn't remember her mom that I hadn't fully considered what I would do if she was. Now I have to figure out what I'm going to do if it comes back that she is my daughter.

Once I'm back in my hotel room, I call Molly. To my surprise, she answers.

"Hey, you," she says, sounding a little groggy.

"Were you sleeping?"

She chuckles. "It's not even late."

"Sorry, I forgot you're three hours behind me." I slump down on the hotel room bed.

"So… what's up?" It's clear she doesn't really understand why I called her.

I'm not even sure I understand it myself. Why, out of everyone, her name came to mind.

"I didn't want to call my family," I blurt out. "I think the little girl is mine."

There's only silence on the other end. Hell, why did I call Molly? So we had sex the other night. We made it clear that neither of us was looking for anything.

"You know what? Forget I called."

"Does that change things?" she asks quickly.

"Well, I mean, yeah. She'll return to Sunrise Bay with me. I'm not sure I'll be much of a father, but I'm also not going to have someone else raise my kid."

"Jed, you do know that you're a good guy, right? Just because you don't want to settle down with someone doesn't mean you can't be a good father."

I take in her words, hoping like hell she's right. "I know."

"I'm not sure you do. That's what you need to think about tonight. How you'll be a good dad."

Her words sink in. "I think you might be the only one who believes in me." My throat feels tight around the words.

She sighs. "The only person who needs to believe in you is you. No one else's opinion matters."

My entire life I've wondered what people thought of

me. Ever since I found out that my dad had been paying off and promising favors to people behind my back to make things happen for me when I was younger.

"Thanks, Molly."

"Just don't tell anyone I said that. I prefer people to think I hate you." She laughs, and it spurs the first smile out of me all day.

"Deal."

"'Night, Jed."

"'Night."

We hang up and I stare at the phone, wishing I had the same confidence in myself that Molly has in me.

Chapter Nine

Jed

The next morning, my cell phone rings next to my bed, waking me since I couldn't get to sleep at a decent hour last night because of the three-hour time difference.

"Hello?" I answer groggily.

"So?"

"Mom, I haven't heard yet. It's supposed to be today. I'll let you know as soon as I do."

I'm ready to end the call, but she keeps talking.

"We're having the annual Greene Summer Bash next weekend. Do you think it would be too overwhelming for her to come? Then again, she has to get to know all of us at some point." I can hear her emptying the dishwasher. The woman is always up at an ungodly hour, finishing all the house tasks before anyone else rises.

"Sure, putting her in front of twenty strangers will be just what she needs."

"I don't need your sarcasm."

I blow out a breath. "Can we please just wait until I find out if I'm even her father?"

No need to mention to Mom the revelation from last night. Not a very proud moment for a mom to hear her son did, in fact, have a one-night stand that he never remembered.

"Fine. But please do not text me when you find out. Call me."

"Okay." I roll onto my back and run my hand through my hair.

"Do you know her name yet?"

I sigh. On the off chance this child isn't my daughter, I don't want my mom to grow mentally attached to her, but I don't have it in me at this early hour to lie. "Her name is Emilia."

"Beautiful name."

There's a long moment of silence. I'm positive she wants to give me some insight for the journey I'm about to embark on. I wait for it, arming myself with the patience to hear her out.

"I love you," she says with what I think might be a clogged throat.

I relax into the mattress. "I love you too. Bye, Mom." I hang up and roll over, flipping the pillow to the cool side and staring at the hotel room.

After trying to go back to sleep and failing, I throw off the covers and head into the bathroom. An hour later, I'm showered, dressed, and eating my breakfast downstairs at the hotel restaurant when David Webb's phone number shows up on my phone.

I take a deep breath and answer his call. "Good morning," I say politely. I haven't made much easy on this guy so far.

"Hiya, Jed. The results are in. Would you like to come into my office this morning? We can square away the details, get the paperwork out of the way, and…"

His voice trails off, giving me the answer I've been waiting for. Emilia is my daughter. David wants to invoke my rights so I can take her back to Alaska with me sooner rather than later.

"So I am?"

He's silent for a beat. "Do you want me to tell you over the phone?"

I stare at my eggs over easy and crispy hash browns. They're half eaten and I'm pretty sure they'll remain that way. Glancing around, I know I'll forever remember this moment. The smell of the hotel restaurant that's a mix of grease and the lavender sprouts in the vase on the table. The old couple by the window with a map spread between them, bickering about where they want to visit today. The little boy who won't stop running around and his father chasing him with threats of discipline. All of this will rush back to me every time I think of this moment. The moment I found out I was a father.

"Yes," I answer.

"Emilia is yours."

Another round of silence. I pick up my napkin, wipe my mouth, place the black fabric on the plate, and push it toward the center of the table.

"I know you might not be ready for this type of responsibility, Jed. When Renee told me she was pregnant with our first child, I was terrified. But don't worry, instinct kicks in. All you have to do is make them feel safe, give them discipline, and love them. Everything else will…"

He continues on, but my head spins as if I might pass out, so I shut my eyes to concentrate on my breathing.

I'm a father.

Responsible for a living, breathing human being.

I can't help but feel sorry for this little girl.

"I'll be at your office in twenty." I hang up and inhale deeply until the spinning sensation passes.

I enter the lawyer's office, but this time, Renee isn't waiting at the desk. Instead, there's a young girl stapling pieces of paper together and typing on the computer, pretending she's talking to someone using her hand as a phone.

"Is David Webb here?" I ask.

She holds up her hand with a stern look and continues asking her hand questions as though she does this every day.

I shove my hands in my pockets and rock back on my heels. What kind of place is David Webb running here?

"Looking forward to seeing you then. Bye now." The girl pretends to hang up her pretend phone hand and still doesn't give me the time of day. Her dark hair is pulled back in braids and she's wearing a purple plaid shirt.

"Excuse me," I say as I lean forward.

She shushes me. Is this David Webb's idea of a trial run? To see how I'll treat Emilia once this is all final?

"I need to see David Webb?" I repeat.

She gives me a fleeting look before she rises off the chair and walks away.

"Great," I murmur to myself.

A few seconds later, Renee comes into view with the little girl at her side. "Bianca, remember I said no stapler." She picks up the pages of white paper that look as if they might have a million staples in them. "Sorry about that. Babysitter called off today and it's an institution day for school."

"I guess these are things I'll have to deal with. Seems wrong to bring her to a bar." My joke falls flat.

Renee glances up from the papers and frowns. "You have a big family, no?" A look must cross my face because she's quick to add, "I mean, David said when he went to your house…"

"Can I ask you a question?"

She looks over her shoulder and back at me. "Sure."

"You were friends with Tanya, right?"

She nods.

"You make Tanya sound like a good person, but how could she not have told me about the pregnancy?"

She looks over her shoulder again and walks out into the small waiting room. Lowering her voice, she leans in. "She didn't come from much and she was scared that somehow she'd be ambushed into living where you're from, or worse, that you'd fight for sole custody."

I would never take a child away from her mother. But she's not wrong that after I wrapped my head around the idea, I would've wanted to be involved in my child's life somehow. How would that have worked? I open my mouth to argue that I'm not that kind of guy.

She raises her hand. "I don't expect someone like you to understand her fear. But she ran away from her own family years before she ever met you. I think she always struggled with her self-confidence. From what I understand in the brief conversations we had about it, she was intimidated by your family."

"How did she even know my name or about my family or where I was from?"

She rolls her eyes. "Unlike you, Tanya wasn't completely drunk all week. She had your name from the credit card statements, and I guess you and your friends kept talking about the small town you were from in Alaska."

I nod because that makes sense. Since Tanya isn't here anymore, I'm going to have to accept that I won't have all the answers I'm looking for. "Thanks."

She steps away but turns back around. "I'm sure eventually Emilia would've asked about her daddy, and she might have reached out."

"But you don't know that for certain."

A scowl transforms her smooth features. "She was a good person, a good mother."

I raise my hands. "I'm not refuting that, but she did keep me in the dark about Emilia. You can't argue that was fair."

She says nothing, and I wait for a retort that never comes. "I'll check on David. Give me a moment."

Then she's gone and walking back to his office. The little girl, Bianca, runs across the hallway into a nearby room and comes out with two juice boxes. Briefly, she looks at me before jetting across the hallway into yet another room. I realize that Emilia is here, and all the air rushes out of my lungs.

My daughter is here. I'm probably about to meet her for the first time. A cold sweat breaks out on my forehead and I wipe it away with the back of my hand.

Renee's only gone a few minutes before she returns and invites me back to David's office.

I stop briefly where I saw Bianca sneak in with two juice boxes, wanting to venture into the office and see my daughter, but I decide to wait, heading into David's office instead. It's time we get down to business.

"So where do we go from here?" I ask, taking a seat.

"There's some paperwork I've already filled out since the paternity test came back positive. We need to go through it all and have you sign some things."

For the next hour, I sign so many papers you'd think I was purchasing a corporation.

"We should have temporary custody worked out so you can return to Alaska in a few days. Then there'll be a final court date, name change, then the granting of full custody to you. The judge will handle all of it. The wait is in getting it all filed and handled, but once we do, it should be pretty simple."

"Name change?"

"I assume you want her last name to be Greene and not Eaton as it is now?"

I lean forward and my head goes into my hands. I hadn't even thought about the fact that her last name hasn't been Greene since she was born.

"Yeah, everything must be written in for the judge to look through." David stacks the papers and puts them in a manila envelope. "Lucky for us both, I have connections, so it hopefully won't be too long."

We sit there and stare at one another. I'm technically looking over his shoulder out the window.

"Would you like to meet her?" he asks after a while. "Maybe the two of you could go to lunch and get to know one another a bit?"

I run my hands down my legs. "Sure. Yeah."

He stands and rounds his desk while I rise from the chair. As I follow him out, my anxiety only increases and I concentrate on breathing so my daughter's first time meeting her dad isn't with me lying on the floor unconscious.

Stopping at the door of the room I assume Emilia is in, David waits a second and looks back at me. I nod to give him the go-ahead, fully aware that if he didn't have a close relationship with Tanya, this whole situation would've gone differently.

He opens the door. Bianca is sitting cross-legged with an iPad propped up against a stack of law books, watching television with Emilia seated next to her. They both look over and I'm pretty sure I stop breathing when Emilia's hazel eyes meet mine.

Everything becomes so real. As though I was looking at a muted picture before and now reality is saturated in color. She's not just a picture anymore. The bloodwork says we share the same DNA. She's a living, breathing little person who is now dependent on me.

"Emilia, this is—"

"Your daddy." Bianca's face lights up when she cuts in and she smiles wide at Emilia.

Emilia just stares at me.

"Go hug him," Bianca says, but Emilia twists around.

"It's okay, Emilia." I try to say it in a soothing voice, but it doesn't seem to help.

Renee runs in. "David, you were supposed to call me before making the introductions." She snatches a now-crying Emilia up in her arms.

I get it, kid. If I was you and saw me as your dad, I'd be crying too.

Chapter Ten

Molly

The bar is crazy, and without Jed around, it kind of sucks. Cade is great and so are my other coworkers, but I hate to admit it's always more fun to work with Jed. He jokes around all the time and it makes my shift go so much faster.

It's tourist season now, so Xavier is helping out since he doesn't do much during football's off-season, except for hang around Clara. Surprisingly though, he's a pro at bartending.

"Are you Xavier Greene?" a woman asks from the end of the bar when he hands a beer to the man next to her.

I laugh and hand a group of seltzers to a guy at the other end of the bar.

"I am." Xavier nods with his winning smile.

"The quarterback for San Francisco, right?" Her eyes light up.

He chuckles and nods again. "That's me."

"And you work here during the off-season?"

The man beside her chips in, "Didn't you just sign some huge five-year deal?"

Xavier's cheeks redden. He's never been the type to bring extra attention to himself. "Yeah."

"And you work here?" The woman has a clear expression of disdain now. I'd love to go over there and ask her what exactly is wrong with working here.

"It's my brothers' brewery," he says and takes their money, cashing them out.

"Oh really? They should have you sign autographs and stuff. Get people in here."

"We're not exactly hurting for business," I interrupt while I pour a draft from the tap.

Xavier snickers while he's filling a beer.

The woman carries on. "I suppose not, but they should have his picture up. It's a huge accomplishment to play professional football."

"So is starting and running your own business." I give her a saccharine smile.

"Millions of people do that, sweetheart, but not many people are professional athletes." She sips her beer.

Xavier walks past me and murmurs, "Let it go."

I do because I know I can get kind of protective of the boys. Besides, this lady doesn't care what I have to say. And it is impressive that Xavier is a professional football player.

We get most of the people waiting at the bar served before Cade comes out and delivers food to a nearby table.

"Who cares what that woman says?" Xavier says, filling up a water to drink.

I shrug. "I know. I'm not sure why I'm being like that."

"You always stick up for Jed. Always have." A customer approaches, so Xavier heads over to take their order while I'm left blinking.

"What's that mean?" I ask when Xavier comes back my way, grabbing a pint glass and filling it up. "I do not."

He laughs. "Yes, you do."

"You stick up for Clara."

"Maybe." He shrugs but doesn't look pleased with my

comment. "You guys have always had some weird thing with protecting one another."

"No, we haven't. I'm his employee and his sister's best friend."

He delivers the drink and leans his hip against the back bar, crossing his thick arms over his chest. "You don't consider Jed a friend after all these years?"

I purse my lips and consider his question. Maybe because I've always seen Jed as unattainable and because I grew close to his sister first, I've never considered that over the years, we've become friends.

"How do you think you got a job here?" Xavier asks.

I open my mouth, but a large group walks through the door and we have no choice but to serve them. But before we greet them, I tug on Xavier's shirt and pull him back. "What do you mean by that?"

He eyes Cade swerving between tables then sighs. "You can't say anything because they'll kill me."

"X? Come on, tell me."

"Cade didn't want to hire you because he thought it might cause issues. That you and Jed might… and that it would end badly, and he'd be stuck cleaning up Jed's mess. But Jed pushed for you. So he obviously thinks of you as a friend." Xavier's eyes widen for a moment, and he steps toward the other side of the bar.

I stand there dumbfounded and a little pissed at the same time. Cade's position annoys me, but I can't help but smile that Jed had my back.

I'm the closer for tonight, since Cade already went home. Xavier and I are about to put the sign to closed when an exhausted-looking Jed walks in through the front door.

"Hey, Dad," Xavier says, joking around.

Jed flips him off and heads to the back office without a word. Xavier goes to the office to talk to Jed while I finish wiping the tables and refilling the saltshakers. Am I buying some time? Absolutely.

I busy myself with wiping down the counters a second time, and double-check the kitchen to make sure the staff cleaned everything properly—Cade's pet peeve.

Xavier steps out of the office as I'm walking out of the kitchen. He pauses, and I catch a glimpse of Jed with his fingers at his temples and his elbows on his desk. Xavier nods for me to follow him out to the seating area.

"He's in bad shape. I promised Marla I'd swing by and grab some election signs to put up around town for her tomorrow. Do you mind making sure he gets outta here with his head on straight?"

Say no, Molly. Say no.

"Sure thing," I say. "Go enjoy some time with Clara."

Xavier stops as he approaches the door and looks at me over his shoulder. "Why'd you say that?"

My eyebrows draw down. "Say what? Clara? I just assumed she'd go with you. You guys spend every waking minute together." I shrug. "You two can't possibly be *just* friends."

Circling around, he looks at me with furrowed brows. "Well, she's not coming."

I put my hands up in front of me. "Okay, if you say so."

He murmurs something under his breath, but he leaves, and I lock the door behind him. I turn off all the lights except the ones over the bar area so the police can see in if they walk by. Break-ins aren't common in Sunrise Bay, but they do trend up during tourist season.

I hear Jed groan as I make my way to his office. He's in the same position he was when Xavier left.

"How are you?" I ask.

He's been gone for three days, but from what Cade said, Jed's daughter, Emilia, returned home with him.

He glances up. "I'm okay."

"Where is she?"

"She's with my mom. I think she hates me." He leans back in his chair.

I step into the room and stand idly by his desk. "No one hates you."

A sinister laugh falls out of him. "What planet are you from?"

So a few people have hated Jed in the past, mostly when he first arrived in Sunrise Bay.

"She's a little girl who just lost her mother. Give her time," I say.

"You know they say kids have a sixth sense, right? She knows I'm going to be a shitty father. I see it in her eyes."

I roll my eyes and sit on the edge of his desk. "You're imagining it."

He rolls his chair toward me and puts his hands on either side of my hips.

"Jeeed," I say with warning in my tone.

Resting his head in my lap, he shakes it back and forth. "Please?" I can't help myself and run my hands through his dark hair, and he moans. "How will I ever get through this and do right by her?"

"You will. Come on. You'll be a great dad. Sure, there's a learning curve, but you'll get through this."

He doesn't move or say anything and I bite my lip.

Then his hands grow tighter and he slides me off the desk, pulling me forward to straddle him.

"Want to come home with me tonight?" he whispers as his lips trail down my neck.

Say no, Molly. Say no.

"Sure." I am the worst. "What about Emilia?"

"She's spending the night at my mom and Hank's. Her decision." I hear the pain in his voice. His fingers fiddle with my belt buckle. "On second thought, let's just stay here, then we'll go back to my place for round two."

"Jeeed."

"It's only us." His lips crash to mine and his tongue dives into my mouth jarringly.

His ferocity takes me by surprise at first. So different from the other night, but it's hot as hell to think he's wanted me this badly while he's been away. Maybe he's been reliving our time together over and over again, consumed with thoughts of how compatible we seemed to be in the bedroom. I know I have.

His hand dips under the waistband of my panties and one finger presses lightly on my clit. "Damn, I missed you."

My heart squeezes while my mind screams, *Do not believe his sweet-talking*. He's no different than any other man.

As I grind along his finger, he pulls his hand out, then both of his hands roam up my shirt to cup my bra-covered breasts. His mouth is on my neck when he picks me up and has me stand. He looks up at me while he pulls my jeans and panties down together, slowly lowering them to the floor. I toe out of my shoes and flick off my socks before stepping out of my jeans, leaving me bare from the waist down.

I reach forward, but he strips off his shirt himself and stands to unbutton his jeans, releasing his rigid bulge. I bite my lower lip, anticipating his girth filling me again.

"Sit on my desk," he says and I do.

He sits back down, swinging my legs over his shoulders, then he rolls forward so his face is inches away from my pussy. He fists his dick in one hand while he runs the pad of his thumb over my clit and down through my wet folds. My back arches and I groan, wanting more.

"Relax, I'll get you there." His voice is low and full of confidence.

When he pushes one finger inside me, I gasp from the intoxicating feeling he provokes more than any man who came before him. Another finger and I bolt off the desk, my ass hanging over, allowing him full access. I stare between my legs and Jed's eyes are on me, brimming with a sinful passion I've never seen before. It undoes something inside me, almost like the chains wrapped tight around my heart are loosening.

He tastes me, stroking then probing, his tongue placing featherlight strokes on my clit. My eyes close and I marvel at his skills because I'm dangerously close to that finish line even though I want this to last longer than a marathon. I never want his tongue or his hands not to be on me again. I clench, trying to hold off my orgasm.

His laughter vibrates along my folds. "Goddamn, I cannot wait for you to squeeze my cock."

"Then what are you waiting for?" My voice is rough, like sandpaper.

"I'm waiting for you to get off on my mouth and fingers." He trails his fingers up and down my slickness.

"Then bury your face in my pussy and get me off." Normally those words would never leave my mouth, but Jed never makes me feel guilty for what feels good.

He chuckles but does just that. His tongue masterfully moves, his fingers plunging, me grinding on his face to get off. He draws my orgasm out of me with an ache so strong, I shudder and goose bumps cover me when I come.

There's no time for me to ride it out because Jed stands, reaches into his desk drawer, and rolls on a condom. "I love watching you come."

He thrusts inside me and I moan, my greedy insides gripping him tightly. His fingers dig into my hips, keeping me steady while everything on the desk jiggles, threatening to fall. We both unravel, quenching our thirst, and he collapses on my chest, beads of sweat along his hairline. I hold his head to my chest, my fingers running through his hair.

I stare at the ceiling, knowing this can't last. If I let it go on much longer, I'm going to be the one who's hurting, just for a different reason than Jed.

Chapter Eleven

Jed

"Fuck." I fall over beside Molly and exhale a deep breath. This woman makes me see stars when I come. She sneaked over last night after Emilia fell asleep and stayed the night at my insistence.

She immediately gets up and gets dressed, adamant that Emilia does not hear or see her. We've kept things between us a secret for a full ten days and I love that she's like me—no strings, just great sex.

"Where's the fire?"

"Emilia could wake up at any time." She throws on her sweatshirt. "I swear I've never been in better shape." She sits on the edge of the bed and puts on her gym shoes.

It's then we hear the creak of the hardwood floor.

Molly looks over her shoulder with an annoyed expression, but there's a knock on my door that springs us both into action.

I fumble with my track pants, shrugging them on. Molly's head whips around, looking from one side of the room to the other, and I swear she looks like she's about to jump out the window before she settles on sliding into the closet.

"Hey, Emilia," Fisher says on the other side of the

door. "I was just going to make some pancakes, want to help me?"

She says nothing.

I don't want Fisher to feel responsible for her, so my hand lands on the doorknob. I had to have a long talk with him once I knew Emilia would be moving in with us. He didn't care, which I thank god for—mostly because I'm scared to be alone with her.

Then Fisher says, "I make Mickey Mouse chocolate chip pancakes. Are you sure you want to pass that up?"

Again, there's no response, but she must give him a nod or something because a second later, he says, "Awesome, let's go."

I hear footsteps on the stairs, so I open up the closet door. Molly pushes me in the chest while I grab a T-shirt.

"I told you I should've gone home last night. Now I have to sneak out with Fisher *and* Emilia downstairs."

She's mad, but it only turns me on. Why do I find it such a turn-on when women get mad at me?

"I'm sorry, I thought we had time."

"You do know that you're going to have to get your act together, right? You can't keep this up," she says, zipping up her sweatshirt and covering the thing I love most about her body—her tits.

I roll my eyes, annoyed that she's jumping on the bandwagon every member of my family is already on. "It's been a week."

"Exactly. A week and she needs you."

"I took her shopping the other day," I say in my defense. "We picked out strawberry shampoo that's supposed to help with the tangles in her hair. I spent a half hour the other day getting her tangles out, which just made her cry."

She shakes her head and sighs. "You have to be gentle.

Ask your sisters, Marla, hell Hank can probably tell you how to do your daughter's hair. He did Chevelle's after Laurie passed."

I throw myself on the bed, wishing I was seven and could cover my ears. "It's so wonderful that everyone has an opinion on my life and how I should handle this hurricane of change."

"Everyone just wants you to grow up and accept the responsibility."

I roll over so I'm on my back. "Easy for everyone else to say. Nothing has changed in their lives."

She stops by the door, and I worry that she's going to stomp out of here pissed off and out us to Fisher. The last thing I need is Nikki catching wind of the fact that I'm boning her best friend. I don't want her on my case.

"Everyone's life changes all the time. You're better than this. You just need to believe it yourself." She opens the door.

"Molly," I whisper.

"Relax, they won't see me." She sounds agitated, as though I tied her to my bed and forced her to stay the night. Hardly, though I did use a little persuasion, mostly with my tongue. Between her legs.

"Hey." I stand and reach for her arm before she gets down the hall. "You're coming to the summer bash, right?"

She pauses in the hallway, staring at me for a beat. "Yeah, I have to talk to Lucy. That girl is hard to get a hold of."

I smile and wink. "Perfect. See you then."

She groans and tiptoes down the hallway. I decide to help the situation and jog loudly down the stairs, then turn to the right to head through the living room into the kitchen while she turns left to go out the front door.

"Good morning," I say, heading to the coffeepot.

Fisher's wearing his uniform again, which means he must've had a late shift. This also means he probably wants to kick my ass because he wanted to go to bed when he got home but decided to save me instead. The scowl he gives me while asking Emilia to drop the chocolate chips into the pancakes confirms my assumption.

"Chocolate chip pancakes, huh?" I ask as though I didn't overhear them.

Emilia doesn't say anything. God, she totally hates me. Never smiles. Only ever answers in nods and headshakes. Occasionally she'll point at something. I heard her talking to my mom the other day, although it wasn't clear and she seemed to be missing words.

Even Fisher seems like he would be a better dad than me, regardless of the fact that he looks like he's dressed up as sheriff for Halloween or something, what with his scruffy beard, shaggy hair, and excess of tattoos that line his arms and poke out above his collar. Emilia isn't afraid of him.

Fisher plates the Mickey Mouse pancakes and carries Emilia to the table. She gets up on her knees on the seat and smiles at the plate. A zing of jealousy zips through my chest like a lightning bolt, leaving searing pain in its wake.

"Can I speak to you?" Fisher asks, and I tear my gaze from Emilia to find a very pissed-off Fisher standing behind her.

"We'll be in the other room," I say to Emilia.

She says nothing, picking up a stray chocolate chip and putting it in her mouth.

Once we're in the other room, Fisher places his hands on his hips like he does when he's questioning a criminal.

"Lay off on the authority act," I say.

"Listen, you wanna fuck random people, go ahead, but

get them out of here before she wakes up. Actually, sleep-overs shouldn't even be a thing for you anymore."

I hold up my hand. "Spare me the lecture."

"Jed, you're playing with a little girl's heart. She lost her mom, you cannot be this much of a dick."

I throw my hands in the air. "I'm not a dick. She's fed, she's clothed, she sleeps in a brand-new bed in her own room."

"It's Adam's old room. And it still has some of his shit that he didn't take with him. Make it a space for her."

Fisher's right. I know he is. There's just been so much to figure out in such a short time. It's overwhelming. I want to be the best dad I can be, but I don't know where to start. This situation feels akin to someone putting me behind the controls of a 747 and telling me I need to fly the plane or we're all doomed.

"I'm doing the best I can. What does everyone expect from me?" I grumble. Not because I think he's wrong, but because that's my go-to when people get on my case. Always has been.

Fisher shakes his head and leans in really close. "We expect you to man the fuck up." Then he walks toward the stairs. "I'm taking a nap before the bash. See you there. Spend some time with your daughter." Then he's gone up the stairs and I hear the click of his door.

Once I'm back in the kitchen, I sit down in front of the coffee cup I left on the table. I watch Emilia eat her pancakes while I wonder how the hell to fill the time before we go to the annual summer bash.

e ended up coloring in some coloring books that my mom had dropped off and going for a short walk through the forest. I didn't take Emilia to the lake because I don't want her to even see that. God forbid she gets curious about it and goes off to check it out herself someday. That water's already claimed one Greene life too many.

Emilia falls asleep on the way over to my mom and Hank's, allowing me to pass her over to my mom, who takes her up to my old room to continue her nap. I pull a beer from the fridge and go out back to join my family. As soon as the first warm weekend rolls around, we all spend it together. Something my mom started as we all kept leaving the house. A way to keep us close, which I'm grateful for now that our family members are starting families of their own.

But I'm not even half finished with my beer when Hank comes out and announces, "Jed, I need to talk to you."

I follow him around the side of the house to the front where the basketball hoop is. He disappears into the garage then bounces a ball to me.

"I really don't—"

"Please, I know I'm not your father, but I refuse to allow your mother to be burdened. She has a lot on her plate with the election and doesn't need to be taking on a grown man's responsibilities."

"She's no—"

He raises his hand and a scowl forms on his lips. "She is. The great thing about being a grandparent is you don't have to be a parent to the child. You don't have to discipline, you get to spoil them. You shouldn't have to think that their father is unfit and try to make it up to the child."

I shoot and miss. "I know. Do you think I don't? I do, but I'm lost."

He sighs, and that seems to douse his ire somewhat. "All I'm saying is I understand how lost you feel but imagine Emilia. Think about her." Hank shoots the ball.

"Fathers usually have nine months to figure this shit out. I had a week to prepare to have a kid. Hank, I'm not the 'number one dad' T-shirt-wearing kinda guy."

"Then be the 'number one dad' mug kinda guy," Hank says.

I blow out a breath, shoot the basketball—missing the shot by five feet—and spot Cade from the corner of my eye. Damn this family. "Am I being ambushed?"

Cade grabs the basketball and dribbles around. "You're not being ambushed," he says, shooting and scoring.

Hank grabs the ball on the rebound.

Cade and Hank are the only ones I'd admit what I'm about to. I put my hands on my hips, my head falling forward in defeat. "I'm gonna fuck her up."

"You're not gonna fuck her up," Cade says.

I peek up through my eyelashes. "My dad fucked me up. Fucked us all up."

Cade throws me the ball and I catch it. "Sure, but we straightened your sorry ass out."

I chuckle because he's right. Eventually I saw the light and came around. Of course, how I'm handling this whole situation makes me think maybe I didn't.

Hank sighs. "Having your mother do all the parenting on your behalf isn't going to make it any easier on you."

I shoot and miss the basket again. "I can't even make a fucking basket."

"You're being way too hard on yourself." Hank grabs the rebound and shoots it. "When Laurie died, I wasn't the best dad I could be. I sulked, and when I was done sulking,

I was yelling because I was so pissed at what the world did to me."

"How could her mother name me on the birth certificate and never tell me? If she'd lived, I never would've known my daughter." And there's another reason I'm struggling so much. "I'm so pissed at her mother, but at the same time, Emilia's suffering from the loss of her." I squat and run my hand through my hair. "I'm so fucking lost. I have no clue what to do."

Cade puts the basketball down and sits on the concrete driveway with me. We had a bumpy ride to become the best friends we are now.

Hank joins us. "It's not gonna be easy, Jed. But you have to put down your walls. Kids don't understand walls. They don't understand guilt-trips and grudges."

It kills me to look him in the eye, knowing the disappointment I've become. Growing up, I didn't have the best role model. My dad was just empty promises because under it all, he was selfish and did whatever he wanted at the expense of his family. I don't want to be my dad, but I fear that maybe it's inevitable.

Cade says, "I know you didn't plan on having a child right now. That you might—"

I look him square in the eye. "I never planned on having kids—ever. I'm not like you, Cade. I don't want a wife or a kid or any of that shit."

Cade looks as if I branded him and the iron rod is still burning his skin.

"You're letting your pain from the past speak for your future." Hank puts a hand on my shoulder.

I shrug it off and stand. "This has nothing to do with my dad. I couldn't give a shit about him. Thanks for the talk, boys, but I got this handled all by myself."

Fuck my family and fuck all this shit.

I sit my ass on the front step of my mom and Hank's house. All the noise from the party out back echoes in the air around me. I'm surprised Emilia can even sleep. Then again, she must be completely zonked out since she rarely sleeps through the night.

I used to spend my nights playing video games, heading to a bar to grab a drink with friends, or generally doing whatever the fuck I wanted. Now I'm tiptoeing around the house, washing tiny clothes, and trying to soothe a girl who looks at me as though I'm the goddamn *IT* clown. The only thing I have going for me is that I'm a killer chef for a three-year-old girl's palate. Mac and cheese, chicken tenders, tater tots—she loves what I feed her. That's the only part I'm winning so far, but even that makes me feel like a loser because shouldn't I be feeding her better stuff?

Does Hank think I *want* to hand over my daughter to my mom?

Hell no, that's not me.

But Emilia sees something in me and I'm pretty sure it's fear. Which does neither of us any good. She's scared because her mom died and she's been left with a stranger, and I'm terrified because I cannot screw her up. I can't. Not when I know what my dad did with my sisters and me and how we're all still living with the repercussions.

The knife to the heart is when Emilia laughs at Fisher. Fisher tickles her, and she laughs. He turns her into a flying airplane, and she laughs. The guy eases the tension well enough, but I swear I think he's better suited than me to be her father.

"What are you doing?" Bibi—which is what I call Ethel, my step-grandmother—comes around the house. "I wondered where you were."

"If you're here to lecture me, your son beat you to it," I grumble and pick up a weed growing through the mulch.

"I don't lecture. You have two other grandmas, you don't need a third."

I cock my eyebrow at her because I consider her my grandma even if it's not by blood. And from what I know, she likes that.

"Okay, so why aren't you enjoying the party?" I help Bibi to sit next to me.

"To tell you a story. When Hank was first born, my husband was so afraid. You know the soft spot on a baby's head and how they're so tiny? He thought for sure he was going to hurt him. He'd say, 'Ethel, my calloused hands will scratch him.'"

I tear the weed into pieces, unsure why she's telling me this. I mean, I get where she's going with it. My entire family is trying to push me in the right direction. And it's not like I'm going to abandon my kid or something, but Jesus, give me a moment to catch my breath.

"I faked sick for an entire week. Pretended I couldn't get out of bed." She chuckles. "He had to cancel all his appointments and take care of Hank for an entire week with no help from me."

"That's kind of evil."

She nudges me with her shoulder. "Nah. After that week, he'd come home and swoop Hank right up into his arms. It's what women who love you will do. Show you how to be the best version of yourself you can be." She winks.

"Well, I don't have a woman, nor do I plan on getting a woman."

Her shoulders fall and she stares at the side of my face because I refuse to face her. "Jed Greene, do not tell me you're one of those bachelors who thinks he's going to be scoring with women half his age when he's old and gray?"

Hell no. I'm not my father. Still, there's no way I'm about to go into all my issues with Bibi right now.

I say, "I'm sure as hell not getting married."

"You have that charm." Her tone is so matter of fact it catches me off guard. "You could probably have any woman you want."

"I'm not sure about that." Tanya Eaton, aka baby mama, clearly didn't think I had what it takes to be a father. Hence the reason she never bothered to tell me she was pregnant.

Grandma Ethel knocks her shoulder against mine again. "You do. All the women down at Northern Lights love you. Always asking about Jed. So easy on the eyes. It's because you compliment them all the time." She nods.

My charisma was inherited from Jeff Greene, my dipshit father. It gets me in trouble. Always has. The other thing that gets me in trouble is my wandering eye. The one that suggests no woman will ever be enough for me, which is why I never wanted kids. I never want to do what my dad did to us.

I shake my head to get rid of the thoughts. "Bibi, I'm friendly. That's all."

"You should go out back and talk to Allie."

I crinkle my brow. "Allie? As in Fisher's Allie?"

"No, she's my Allie. Actually, Dori's I suppose, since we were fixing up Kingston when we met her." She looks as confused as I am.

"The only Allie I know, and the one who's at this party, is Fisher's friend."

Her gray eyebrows scrunch together, and I see her wheels turning. If I'm lucky, they'll turn right around to fixing up Fisher and Allie and she'll get off my back.

"Huh," Bibi says. "Regardless, do you really want that sweet little girl to grow up without a mommy figure?"

I bury my head in my hands, massaging my temples with my fingers. "Fucking hell. I love you, Bibi, but I can't have this conversation right now." A man can only take so much.

Chapter Twelve

Molly

When I arrive at the summer bash, Jed is playing basketball with Cade and Hank. He doesn't spot me, which is fine. The last thing I need is him to distract me from talking to Lucy. Professor Locklear told me that I only have a short window to find a new child, otherwise I'm out of luck. Besides, it's about time I put myself before a man.

"*Mol!*" Nikki screams. "About time. What happened to the solidarity of a one-piece?" Her voice turns sinister, and everyone laughs.

Oh yeah, I was supposed to wear a one-piece, but I don't own one.

"Sorry, but you're rocking your swimsuit."

She's wearing a swimsuit with red palm trees that show her growing belly. She looks adorable, and because Logan is rubbing sunblock on her back, she looks as if she's in heaven.

"I should've worn the one that said save the whales. I feel like a beached whale."

I laugh and toss my bag on the empty lawn chair by Nikki, leaving on my cutoff jean shorts. There are some new faces I've never seen before, most notably the brunette talking with Fisher. He's usually not one for publicly flirting. He's much more an after-hours kind of guy—I think because he's the sheriff and all.

"Who's the dark-haired girl?" I whisper to Nikki.

"Allie. Ethel wants to set her up with Cam or Jed, I think?"

My stomach drops. "What? Why?"

"Because she and Dori claim they're, like, match-makers or something. I don't know." She waves me off, then moans as Logan's hands massage her.

"I'm fully disgusted by the sounds coming out of you," Mandi says next to Nikki.

"Don't be jealous. He can do you next if you'd like," Nikki says.

Mandi's eyebrows hit her forehead. As do Logan's.

"Babe," he says.

"What? You know what I meant. He can put sunscreen on you. Not like we're going to be sister wives or some-thing. Jeez, you guys." Nikki sounds as exhausted as she looks. Not the best endorsement for pregnancy, that's for sure.

"Did Jed seem interested?" I ask as nonchalantly as I can manage.

Nikki's head flings in my direction, her gaze glued to me as though I'm about to confess what I've been doing with him.

"Please, that boy is lost. He barely knows she's here," Mandi says.

Nikki's now squinting at me. Shit, my question has put up her little gossip antennae.

"What?" I ask to divert the attention.

"You had that worried sound in your voice."

I shake my head and act as though she's crazy. "Not at all. I was just curious." I lean forward. "I mean, we all know where Cam's intentions lie." I glance over at Chevelle sunbathing in a tiny bikini.

She nods and Mandi agrees too.

"You good?" Logan asks. "Sounds like the girl talk is starting and I'd rather not be part of it."

We all laugh, and he bends down, kissing his wife. I smile because my best friend deserves a guy like him. Someone completely smitten with her.

"Go play with your friends," Nikki says.

"Nik!" I groan.

"What? I just meant volleyball in the pool or something." She looks at me a little longer than usual. "You remember freshman year, right? What my brother did to you?"

Damn it, I'm the one who tossed her the bone she can't stop chewing on.

I lean forward in my chair. "Mandi, tell her she's imagining things."

"Come on, Nik, you know as well as I do, she'd never fall for his antics again." Mandi nudges her sister, straightening in her chair and picking up her magazine.

"I sure hope so. I'd hate if I had to make sure he never had a second kid." Nikki sips her water and closes her eyes, soaking up the sun.

As we all lie there, my mind travels back to that football game and the two of us behind the concession stand.

Jed had said to meet him a half an hour before the game was to start.

No one was really around except for a sprinkling of parents who always got there early for the game.

I paced, wondering if I'd made the right decision, but even if I'd had doubts, it would've been too late. Jed arrived with a flashy smile and his hot body moments later.

"Hey, you," he said with a nod that made his hair float up and down.

"Hey."

He grabbed my hips. "I don't have a ton of time, but after the game, we can go somewhere if you want."

I swore my insides lit up like a full moon. "Sure, there's a pizza place—"

But he tugged me to him, cutting me off. "I like this." He ran a hand down the braid that was resting on my shoulder. "A lot."

I nodded, unsure how to respond.

Then he turned us flawlessly and my back was against the old wood of the concession stand and he stepped closer to me. "You're all I've thought about all day."

Jed bent forward and placed his lips on mine. He slipped his tongue in my mouth. I'd only ever French kissed one other boy, so I hoped I didn't come off too inexperienced.

His hands inched up, and one molded to my breast through the thin fabric of my sweater. His thumb ran along my nipple and I remember thinking that he must've already had sex before because of how confident he was. It was my first time being felt up, but it felt so good. The smell of him, like fresh soap, wrapped me up in a bubble. I was kissing Jed Greene, the guy every girl wanted.

He ended the kiss and I leaned forward, not wanting it to end. He chuckled at me.

"I gotta go. Coach will have my ass if I'm not back soon. I'll find you after the game." He winked and ran toward the locker room.

But he never did find me, and after the game, I saw him opening his truck door to help in a senior cheerleader. Tears pricked my eyes, and I couldn't stop them from falling as I watched him drive off. One by one, all the football players left, and I stood in that dark parking lot by myself. I'd already told Melanie I had a ride home and she'd left.

A van stopped near me and a blonde teenage girl popped her

head out. "I know you don't know me, but my mom wants to know if you need a ride?"

I knew if I didn't accept this ride, I was screwed. And although I assumed they were from the opposing team, I climbed in, thankful I wouldn't have to walk home since my mom was out on a date.

"Thank you," I said, climbing in.

There were two red-haired girls in the back seat.

"Are you okay, sweetie?" the mom asked, looking at me in the rearview mirror.

"Yeah." I wiped the remaining tears from my cheeks.

The mom, who I later learned was Marla, insisted I go for pizza with them. She wouldn't take no for an answer, and pizza always helped when you were feeling down, so I agreed. They had so much fun on the way over, singing and making jokes. The littlest one, Posey, showed me how she'd cut her Barbie's hair. It was more fun than I'd had in a while and I couldn't believe there were families like this out there.

I had hoped that Jed went somewhere other than the pizza place with his new girl, but when we walked into the restaurant, sure enough, he was there at the football table with Reese's best friend by his side. He didn't even give me a fleeting look.

"You good?" the blonde, Nikki, asked.

"Yeah. I just saw the asshole who used me, that's all." I narrowed my eyes at him.

"Which one?" There was a hitch in her tone.

"The one at the head table, holding court."

"He used you? How?"

At that point, I sensed something and looked at her, brows drawn. "Why?"

"Because that's my brother. I'm Nikki Greene."

My mouth fell open. "I need to go. Tell your mom thank you."

I turned to walk out, knowing I could make it home from here, *but I wasn't out the door for more than thirty seconds before Nikki called my name.*

She jogged to catch up to me. "Wait. Listen. My brother is a douche. He uses people. Come back in, have pizza."

"I don't want him to see me," I said.

She smiled. "The best thing you can do is act as though it meant nothing to you. Plus, now that we're friends, you're forbidden from him anyway. Best torture ever."

"We're friends?" I asked.

She slid her arm through mine. "Yep, and I'm not taking no for an answer. My brother's loss is my gain."

I smile as the memory fades. I grab Nikki's hand and lay my head on her shoulder.

"What's all this about?" she asks.

"Thank you for befriending me all those years ago."

"Thanks for letting me bulldoze you into a friendship." We both laugh.

Lucy walks by and it pulls my attention away.

"Luce!" I shout.

She stops and laughs at me. "I'm right here. No need to yell." She sits down on the lounger with me. "What's up?"

I explain the situation with my clinical and I see the frown on Nikki's lips, the concern in her eyes.

Lucy purses her lips and seems to think for a moment. "I can definitely ask around. It's just so late in the year, you know? I have a feeling I won't find anyone."

I lean back in the chair. I knew it would be hard to find someone. Might as well plan on graduating in December. "Thanks, Lucy."

"Sure. I will check though, so don't lose hope yet."

Just then, Marla walks out of the house with Emilia plastered to her chest.

"I could kick my brother in the nuts for what he's doing. Or not doing, I should say." Nikki's voice is filled with disgust.

Marla sits in a chair, running her hand up and down her granddaughter's back.

"You know…" Lucy begins but doesn't finish.

"What?" I turn in her direction.

She nibbles on the inside of her cheek. "It's not really my place, but the other day I was over and Emilia was here. She rarely talks, but when she does, I did notice that it's not a lot of words. I'm not sure if she knows them and isn't saying them, but if it is the extent of her vocabulary, she's behind."

I look at Marla and close my eyes. The last thing I need is for my clinical to be with Jed's daughter. It'd further complicate things between us. I'm not sure he'd allow me to try to help anyway.

"Perfect," Nikki says. "You know Jed will say yes. Actually, just ask my mom for permission since Jed's an absentee dad these days anyway."

"Relax, Nik," Mandi says from next to her. She's the sweet Greene—the people pleaser who hates confrontation.

"You know it too, Mandi. The guy just waltzes around breaking hearts and thinking he's had a hard life. Please. He had all of Dad's attention, plus anything else he wanted. It's called adulthood. He should look it up in the dictionary."

"I'm going to grab a drink," I say, sliding off the lounge chair and heading toward the food.

I know why Nikki feels the way she does about her brother and what it's doing to her mother, but I don't think Nikki understands the sheer amount of fear Jed has.

I round the house and find Jed walking in my direction, coming from the front of the house.

"Hi." He approaches me.

"Emilia is fast asleep in your mom's arms," I tell him.

His eyes focus on my breasts and his lids grow heavy. I'll never grow tired of the lust in his eyes. He glances around to make sure no one is nearby, then he takes my hand and guides me back toward the front of the house.

We watch Ethel's back as she goes the other way around the house, then Jed opens the front door and sneaks us into his family home.

Chapter Thirteen

Molly

Nikki would kill me if she knew I've been fooling around with her brother. It's not like this is anything serious between us. It's two grown adults having fun together. Pure lust and pleasure. It wasn't my plan to come here today and entice him, but I see the stress he's under. I just want the happy Jed to come back. No harm, no foul, right?

"Come on," he whispers and guides me up the stairs to what I think was Posey's bedroom once upon a time.

Quietly, he shuts the door. The voices from the party drift up to the second floor, but it's as though Jed doesn't hear them because his hands land on my face and his lips on mine in seconds. His tongue dives into my mouth and I meet his eagerness with a ferocity of my own.

"You're killing me in this thing," he says, his fingers making quick work of my bikini top. Then his hands are on my breasts, massaging, twisting, teasing my nipples. "You did it on purpose. Just to turn me on."

"No," I lie, because of course I did. I feel as though I've been dressing for him for most of my life. It's pathetic, I'm aware.

"Liar. It only makes me want you more."

"Then yes, I did."

His hands grow firmer, tightening on my breasts. The feeling of him touching me sends an electrical jolt down my body, centering between my thighs.

"I knew it. Why can't I get enough of you?" His face dives into my neck and his tongue slides up to my ear. His heavy breathing in my ear is like he's strumming my clit. I grow wet from the sound.

"I'm not sure we should be doing this here." My intention with wearing this bikini was so he'd call me later tonight after Emilia falls asleep. I thought we'd flirt a little today—like foreplay—during the barbecue, then we'd seal the deal when there were no witnesses around.

"Fuck it. They're all busy." His hands slide under the back of my bikini bottoms, pushing me into him so his long, hard length hits my stomach. Damn, the man is talented, I'll give him that. "Busy with their damn perfect lives."

I still.

He tears off his shirt. The man has abs I could definitely clean my soaked bikini bottoms on. Then he's opening his board shorts, taking my hand and putting it on his dick. "See what you do to me?"

God, how long have I waited for those words to come from his mouth?

I stroke him, and his eyes close briefly. "Damn, that feels good."

The more I'm in this room, looking at Posey's prom pictures and all her girly items from high school, the more off it feels. What happens when I leave this room?

I'm back to being Molly, Nikki's best friend, for the rest of the night.

"Jed?" I say.

His hand slides down the front of my bikini bottoms

and his fingers dive between my folds, playing with my clit. "Uh-huh?"

"I don't think it's a good idea if we do this heere. Maybe I can come by tonight."

His lips are on my skin now as his fingers play with me, making it hard to fight him.

"I don't want a booty call tonight, I want it now," he says in a low voice.

"And that's all this is, right?"

There must be something in my tone I didn't hear because he rears back, and his hands slip from under my bottoms. He stares at me long and hard. "Don't tell me you're gonna make things complicated now?"

There's anger lacing his tone. Anger I've never heard from Jed before.

"Should I just spread my legs when you say go?" I snipe.

Sometimes lately—after Emilia got here—when he looks at me, it's no longer the same Jed. He's lost some-where, and I have no idea where or how to help him escape the trap he's put himself in.

"I thought we agreed to no strings?"

"We did," I say.

A cocky smile forms on his lips. He approaches me, and for a moment, I allow myself to be his distraction. What's the harm? I don't have feelings for Jed Greene. At least not anything more than lust. Ugh. Even I know I'm lying to myself.

A knock on the door sounds and I push Jed off me, but he must be drunk on lust because he comes right back as though I'm playing some game. He grabs my ass and pulls me toward him.

"Jed?" a deep male voice says, and Jed freezes. "Oh shit."

Fisher's eyes pierce into mine when I look around Jed's large body.

"Get the fuck out," Jed says, whipping his head toward his brother.

Fisher's face falls and he shuts the door. Then we hear laughter.

"Oh my god, he won't tell Nikki, will he?" I grab my bikini top off the floor to fasten it back on. "She'll kill me."

"What are you doing? Fisher won't say anything. Keep that off." Jed reaches for my bikini top, but I manage to get dressed and slide away from him.

"I think this was a bad idea."

"So now you're gonna bail on me?" Jed sits on the edge of the bed, his board shorts still open.

I step forward but manage to keep myself far enough away from him. We never should have started whatever this is between us.

"Just go, Molly," he says.

I leave, but mostly to tell Fisher that if he speaks a word of this, I'm coming after him with a meat grinder.

Sneaking down the stairs, I hear Nikki talking from somewhere in the house and guilt weighs heavy on my heart. I'd never want to risk our friendship, but maybe Nikki would be cool with me dating her brother.

I shake my head. What the hell am I thinking? Jed Greene's been emotionally unavailable my entire life. Nothing's changed. In fact, it's worse.

J begged Fisher not to say a word, then I spent exactly one more hour at the bash before making an excuse to leave. I didn't make eye contact with Jed once after I left the bedroom, which wasn't that hard since he didn't even come out of the house for a half hour after. At least he did sit next to Emilia and his mom. Even fixed his daughter a plate.

Now, I'm crouched on the main road that goes through Sunrise Bay, jacking up my car to replace a flat tire, when all I really want is to bury myself under my blankets at home.

I hear a car slow next to me and I peek over my shoulder to see a Cadillac. The Cadillac that the Greenes' grandmother, Ethel, drives around town with her blue-haired friend Dori and, on occasion, the kleptomaniac Midge. Dori rolls down her window.

"Do you need some help? I could call one of my grandsons," Ethel screams.

The last person I need is one of the Greenes, especially not Jed, coming to help me like I'm some damsel in distress.

I smile. "No, thank you. I can change a tire."

I turn back to continue on because if they've left the party, I'm sure others will be on their way too and there's no way Nikki would let Logan drive by without helping. Then who knows who else might join in? I love the Greenes, they've showed me what family means, but tonight I just want some solitude to reprimand myself for starting anything with Jed in the first place.

But the Cadillac idles next to me, the occupants watching my every move.

As I'm putting the jack away, thankful I finished with just this small audience, Ethel screams out the window once again. "How would you like to have a drink with Dori and me?"

Say no, Molly. Say no.

"Um… sure."

I can't say no to two grandmas. It just feels wrong.

"Great. Follow me to this place in Lake Starlight called Lucky's." She pulls over on the shoulder in front of me to wait for me to get in my car.

I groan. Lake Starlight isn't that far, but it's farther than I would've liked to go tonight. But Ethel's always been good to me. Maybe she wants to plan some surprise shower or something baby related for Nikki. So I climb into my car and follow them out of town.

We arrive at Lucky's, which is located in the small downtown area of Lake Starlight, meaning it's street parking only. While Ethel parks in the one handicapped spot in front of Lucky's, I end up farther down the street, but we all end up at the front door at the same time.

I glance at the Cadillac and see Midge asleep with her mouth open in the back seat.

"Um… what about Midge?" I ask.

They turn to look as if they forgot her.

"She'll be fine. We cracked the windows." Dori smiles.

"She's not a dog. It's dark and—"

"This is Lake Starlight." Ethel shrugs.

"Even so, it's tourist season." I look at Midge again. She looks very comfortable leaned against the window, and the windows are indeed cracked open.

Dori pulls out her phone. "I'll call Sheriff Miller and have him do some drive-bys. Does that appease you?"

"Sure…"

While she's on the phone, Ethel swoops her arm through mine. "Come on, let's go inside."

I've been here only a few times, since I much prefer Truth or Dare Brewery. There's pool tables and dart boards in one corner, and wooden booths and a long bar on the other side of the room. The music is louder than we play it at the brewery, but it fits the vibe of the place.

As I'm sliding into an empty booth, the entire place screams, "Dori!"

She waves as she comes through the door like Miss America and joins Ethel on the other side of the booth.

"You're like a celebrity here. Are any of your grandchildren here tonight?" I ask.

She peeks around the edge of the booth. "They shouldn't be. They all have kids of their own now." Her hand goes up and a guy with a scruffy beard and blond hair comes over. "Hi, Nate."

I'm not surprised she knows him by name.

Nate says, "Hey, Dori. Ethel. Missing your friend Midge tonight?"

"Oh no, she's in the car," I say, and I swear Dori rolls her eyes at me. I'm pretty sure Dori would have something to say if they left her in the car.

"She's fine. I called the sheriff." Dori waves me off.

Nate laughs as though he's used to this type of behavior. I'll take it as a warning that I might not want to hang out with these ladies very often.

"What can I get you guys?" he asks.

They each order an iced water, and I tilt my head at them.

"We're old, Molly, we can't be ruining what little liver function we have left." Ethel smiles and pats my hand. "But you order whatever you want."

I glance at the bar to see what they have on tap, and I'm surprised to find Razzle Dazzle from Truth or Dare. "You have Razzle Dazzle?"

Nate nods. "We're trying it out. You from Sunrise Bay?"

"Yeah, and I work at Truth or Dare."

"What are you doing here then?"

I nod toward the two old ladies across from me.

He adds, "Watch out, nothing good comes when they bring people here."

"Oh hush, Nate, go get our drinks," Ethel says.

He looks at me to confirm I want the Razzle Dazzle.

I nod. "Thank you." After he goes to the bar, my eyes follow him. "He's a cute guy."

Ethel and Dori look at one another in question before locking gazes on me.

I rear back in the booth because of the intensity of their gazes. "What?"

"Tell us about yourself," Dori says.

I eye Nate to see how quickly he's going to get my drink. I have a feeling I'm going to need it.

Chapter Fourteen

Jed

Once the summer bash calms down, I take Emilia home.

She's quiet as usual, but she always seems especially quiet with me. I remember Rylan at her age and I swear he never stopped talking.

I park the truck in the driveway and unhook her from the car seat I'm now a pro at. After she woke up from her nap, she wanted to go in the pool, so I'm not surprised to find her head drooping.

Hank's words ring in my ear, "Imagine how Emilia is handling this." I've been so caught up in my own shit and worrying about being a crap dad that I'm being a crap dad. It's unacceptable.

I lift her and her arms droop over me, her head leaning on my shoulder. She doesn't cling to me like she does my mom, and if I'm honest, it upsets me. But maybe I don't deserve that small token of affection from her when I haven't been openly displaying mine at all.

Although she should probably have a bath, I suppose it can wait until tomorrow.

"Mama," she says when I lay her on her bed, her eyes barely open. "Mama!" Her voice grows louder, her arms lifting and her fists clenching.

It feels as if my sternum is collapsing in on itself as I witness her distress. "Shh… Emilia, it's me. Let's get you dressed so you can go to bed."

I quickly change her into a pair of pajamas. Her eyes open, and the disappointment that it's me and not her mom is evident. She wants her mama, and to be honest, I want mine too. My mom is just so much more adept at handling this.

The door downstairs opens. Fisher's big footsteps come up the stairs, and when they stop, I glance over my shoulder and see him leaning against the doorframe.

He left soon after finding Molly and me. He and Allie said they were going for a walk around the town square, but I knew he had to get out of there before laying into me in front of everyone and outing Molly's and my extracurriculars.

"We need to talk when you're done." He pushes off the doorframe. "'Night, Emilia."

She doesn't say much, grabbing her stuffed ostrich, which if you ask me looks grumpy and not comforting at all, but from how beat up it is, I'm guessing she's loved it a long time.

"Good night," I say, tucking her under the blankets and rising to my feet.

She rolls over to face the wall, and I turn on the star galaxy lamp I got her since the store was out of nightlights. I always wanted a nightlight when I was little, so I assumed she might too. After shutting the door, I walk downstairs, ready for the wrath of Fisher, but I hear a feminine voice that throws me. When I reach the bottom of the stairs, I see Chevelle and Cam on my couch.

"Where's Fisher?" I ask.

"He's in the kitchen, but—" Chevelle starts.

I want to clear the air immediately though, so I hold up

a finger and head into the kitchen to find him. He turns from the fridge with four beers in his hands and offers me one. I take it and open the bottle, then take a sip of it.

I touch his arm with my free hand and he stops. "Can we talk?"

"Don't worry, I won't say shit, but I hope you know it's gonna blow up in your face. Nikki's gonna find out. Molly's gonna get hurt."

"It's over. She ended it." I ignore the pinch in my chest when I say the words.

He looks unimpressed. "How are the two of you going to work together now?"

I shrug. "We've been walking that line for years. It was bound to happen at some point."

"Convenient though." Both his eyebrows rise and I'm thrown for a moment.

My forehead wrinkles. "What does that mean?"

He shakes his head and gives me a disappointed look. "It means that you were thinking with your dick. You forgot all the strings that messing around with Molly brings." His voice is low, so Cam and Chevelle won't overhear from the living room.

"She said—"

"You're a moron. She's Nikki's best friend. She's wanted you since your sorry ass moved here. She comes to almost every family function. She's treated like a family member by my dad and Marla since her own mother doesn't really give one shit about her."

I slump down into one of the kitchen chairs, taking in everything he's saying.

"All I'm saying is sometimes you only think of what's good for Jed and not what's good for anyone else. If Molly doesn't have the Greenes or her job at Truth or Dare, where do you think that leaves her?"

I shake my head because I don't have an answer. I thought Molly and I were on the same page until I saw the hurt in her eyes tonight when she asked if she was just a booty call. I never intended to make her feel that way, but I thought that she understood that I couldn't do… more.

"You've been sneaking her in here when you should've been being a fucking father."

"Goddamn it. I'm so sick of everyone and their damn opinions. Do you have a kid you don't know upstairs? One who looks at you like you're a monster? Is your entire life up in the air? No."

He chuckles and shakes his head. "Do you know what it's like to lose your mother? Talk about having your entire life up in the air."

I swallow the lump forming in my throat. Fisher has a point.

"I thought you were done thinking only about yourself. But as soon as the perfect life you thought you had gets messy, you're back to being the boy you once were and not the man you'd become."

Jesus, that comment hurts.

He leaves the room before I can say anything, though I'm not sure I have anything to say to that anyway. Fisher, like the rest of my stepsiblings, lost his mom and knows exactly what my daughter is going through.

Sometimes I thought I knew, since I pretty much lost my dad as soon as I didn't agree to live my life by buying everything I wanted, but it's not the same. I barely talk to the man at all, but if I wanted, I could pick up the phone and call. They can't.

Hell, my dad must've heard about Emilia from one of my siblings because he's called a few times over the past week, but I send him straight to voice mail. I have enough to deal with right now without adding him to the mix.

Sitting at the table, I massage my temples with my fingers.

"Hey, Jed," Chevelle says, and I look up to find her staring at me.

"Hi, Chevelle." I lean back in the chair and sip my beer.

She hesitantly joins me, laying the box on the table. "I wondered if I could talk to you for a second?"

Chevelle is the youngest of Hank's children, and truth is, I was out of the house before I really got to know her as a child. I know her more as the adult with a kick-ass attitude who's not afraid to speak her mind. And so, I gear myself up for another lecture I know I deserve.

"What's up?"

She laughs. "Don't sound so enthused."

"It's not that. I've been lectured about twenty times tonight. I know I'm a shit dad."

She sits down and uses her shirt to crack open her beer. "You're not a shit dad. You're a *new* dad. Give yourself a break."

"Thanks." I give her a weak smile.

"But…"

I groan. She laughs, shifting her blonde hair from one shoulder to the other.

"When I lost my mom, it was so hard. I feel a kinship with Emilia."

I nod.

"My dad was all about the boys. Sure, he loved me. I never thought otherwise, but he kind of handled the boys and my mom handled me. She and I would go late to my brothers' games or she'd be the one to help me ice skate while my dad played pond hockey with the boys. Maybe because I was younger, but maybe because I was a girl too." She shrugs.

I've never asked Chevelle if she harbors any guilt about how her mother died—because Chevelle had wandered out onto the pond's thinning ice. I can't seem to get my act together after how my father imploded our family, so I'd have to guess that she must. Even if she was only five when it happened.

Jeez, that's only two years older than Emilia.

"I know we all look at my dad as the wise, all-knowing one in the family these days, but it took him so long to get his act together. Poor Cade tried to do my hair at first for the special occasions, you know? Grandma tried too, but all I wanted to do was hole myself in my room and act like my mom was downstairs. When the people I'd known my whole life tried to bring me into the fold and fill the spot my mom left behind, I resisted. I can't imagine what it's like for Emilia when she didn't even know you existed until after her mom passed away. I know you might doubt yourself, Jed, but in doing so, you're only proving yourself right."

"I get what you're saying." I take a pull of my beer.

"By being scared that you can't handle it, that you're going to be your father, you're turning into that dad. It's a self-fulfilling prophecy. Come on, we both know you're better than that. The way you were with Posey and me back in the day? Hell, look at Rylan."

"I wasn't responsible for you full time. I was the fun brother. Throwing you in a pool, playing games. That stuff is easy and comes naturally to me. But I'm responsible for making her into a good human being. To be there for her, shelter, feed, and nurture her. That's what I'm scared of. I've never been Mr. Responsibility."

Chevelle nods and her soft hand lands on mine. "I know. I think my dad was scared too. He eventually came out of his anger and denial phase, but right now, this very second, that little girl needs someone to love her more than anything else."

"I'm not even sure she wants me to love her."

"Because you're not letting her in. You've erected a wall between you and she feels it. Hug her. Kiss her. I know you love her just because of the fact that she's your daughter. Your flesh and blood."

I do love Emilia, but that gets pushed aside when the anger at Tanya roars to life. I should've been part of Emilia's life from the get-go. Or when the doubt that I'm not good enough to be her father consumes me.

"It doesn't take much at this age, Jed. Just transparency. Love her. Do your best and stop worrying so much about whether it's good enough, and it will all fall into place. Give her time to heal. I'm sure she doesn't understand and misses her mom a lot, but you're the adult. This all starts with you. Show her the Jed we all know and love. The one who brings humor into a tense situation. The one who protects his family with fierce loyalty. Show her what a great dad you are."

Maybe I'm expecting too much too soon from Emilia. It's not her job to prove to me that I'm being a good father by fawning over me with affection. It should be the other way around.

I finish off my beer and nod. "Okay. I will." My voice is infused with raw determination. The pity party is over. It's time to step up and deal with the situation as it is, not what I wish it could be.

"Promise?"

I wonder if anyone coerced her to come here and talk sense to me. "Yes. I promise."

"So tomorrow, you start by taking her to the zoo or somewhere little girls want to go... maybe talk to Posey and see if her girl at the salon can paint her nails or take her shopping for some clothes. Distract her and let her get to know you. That's probably the best thing Hank ever did. He started having daddy-daughter days with me. The days only me and him would do something, just the two of us."

I smile at her. "Thanks, Chevelle."

She gets up from the table. "No problem. It sucks that it's my expertise, but I had to learn early, just like Emilia, that life isn't a smooth road." Her frown pierces my heart. "Now I have to go kick Cam's ass at *Mario Kart* because he called me out at the party."

She walks out, and a second later, I hear the razzing and arguing between the two of them.

I throw my beer in the trash and head upstairs. I check on Emilia once before going to my room to go to sleep because a good dad wakes up before his daughter.

Chapter Fifteen

Molly

I stare at both women across the booth.

"Well, you know I'm Nikki's best friend," I say, as though I have to remind them. After all these years, I'm not sure why they feel the need to get to know me.

"We know that." Ethel laughs. "What are your dreams? Aspirations? Any boyfriend in the picture?"

Thankfully, Nate brings over our drinks and I have the glass to my lips just as Dori says we should cheers. I'm not sure what we're celebrating, but I swallow the sip I already had in my mouth and put my drink in the air in the middle of the table.

"To new beginnings," Dori says, and both women clink their glasses of water to my beer.

"Now back to you, dear." Ethel doesn't sip her water, but places it on the table.

"Um… I'm going to grad school for speech pathology. Supposed to graduate this semester. After that I hope to secure a job somewhere, ideally a school."

They both nod and wait for more. Okay, that's not enough information for them. What else have I got?

"That's basically my dreams and aspirations. And no boyfriend."

"Do you want a boyfriend?" Ethel asks.

Based on the fact that they're asking more about my love life and not my career aspirations, I can see which way this conversation is going. "No, I don't."

"You don't want a boyfriend?" Dori glances at Ethel as though I'm crazy.

"Well, I wouldn't mind a nights-only boyfriend, if you get my gist." Let's see what these ladies think of that.

"Scandalous," Dori says. "Back in my day, if a girl said that she'd gain a reputation."

"Been there, done that, and I'm over it." I say that, but thinking about it stings just the same. "Call Molly Monroe for a blow" will forever haunt my memory. The fact that I sorta lived up to that name after it was wrongly given to me doesn't help.

"Oh really? Do tell." Ethel places her chin in her palm.

I open my mouth but shut it. "Why? Why do you ladies want to know all this stuff about me?"

"We love Nikki and she loves you," Ethel says sweetly.

"With all due respect, ladies, I call bullshit."

Both women look at one another. I expect them to hightail it out of here, to be offended by what I said, but they laugh, nod, and set their attention back on me.

"We like you," Dori says.

"Thanks. I like me too."

"Back to the boyfriend thing. If you have the right boyfriend, you can have all the fun in the sheets you want *and* a warm heart." Ethel's eyebrows shoot up to her hairline.

"I'm not really a marriage type of person, and boyfriends tend to lead to marriages at my age."

Dori quirks her lips. "In this day and age, you definitely don't need to get married."

She has a point, so I nod. "You don't, but what's truly the difference if the boyfriend thing gets serious and you move in together? Same thing." I shrug and pick my beer back up for a sip.

"And why are you against it?"

"Why do you want to know?" I ask Ethel back. If I'm laying out all my cards, they better lay out theirs too.

She looks at Dori as though she needs permission. "We're old and like to use what time we have left wisely. To help guide the younger generation down the right path."

Impressive she came up with a way to spin her reputation for being a meddler so fast, but the truth is that I'm tired of holding everything in. I can't talk to my best friend about it, so I see no problem in getting their advice on what just transpired with Jed—without them knowing it's him I'm talking about.

"I don't believe in monogamy. I don't think that one person will ever be faithful."

Their jaws fall open for a second, then they both shrug.

"You're not the first," Ethel says.

"That's good to know." I sip my beer and crack my neck.

"You seem so stressed." Ethel's hand lands on mine, squeezing it once. "You can talk to us."

And just like that, with two grandmas I know are nosy, who get involved in so many things that don't pertain to them, their caring natures have me spilling it all.

"I just couldn't do it, you know? Be used anymore. I know I agreed and he's probably mad, which, whatever…" I wipe tears off my cheeks but more replace them. "All I want to do is graduate, and now that's a huge fiasco because I have to find another child who could use my help and Lucy doesn't know anyone. So I'm stuck there too." My head falls to the table with a thud, and I'm met with silence for a beat.

"Oh dear." Dori sounds unsure how to handle me. I certainly can't be the first person to lose it in front of them.

I sit up and wipe the tears. "But I'm good. I'm fine. I don't need him. If he doesn't know how special I am, then screw him, right?"

"Right," Ethel says. "Who is he though?"

I stop talking and the tears dry up. I can't very well tell her who he is. They wouldn't understand. "It doesn't matter. Listen, it's been really nice and thanks for letting me cry on your shoulders, but I should get going."

I pull out some money and put it on the table, but Dori's hand lands on mine. "Can we help you with your school problem at least? Surely between all of us there's someone we can find to help you out. I have a ton of great-grandbabies. I can get one of them to make up a problem if we need to."

I chuckle. "No. I don't want any children having to fake a speech impediment."

Dori looks at Ethel. "What about…"

Ethel's eyes flare and light up. "I think I know someone. Can you meet us at Northern Lights Retirement?"

"Wait, do you really know someone?"

Ethel and Dori are known for their tactics of setting people up. I have no idea who they'd even be trying to hook me up with, but from what I saw, they're a little off the mark. I mean, trying to set up Cam with that woman Allie? It was clear tonight she's only got eyes for Fisher, and hello Cam? Everyone knows there's only one woman who turns him on.

Ethel nods. "I do. I promise. Why don't you put your number in my phone and I'll contact you with a day and time?"

She slides her phone across the table, and I hesitate before picking it up. "You can't share my number."

She laughs. "Never."

I nod and type in my number, saving it as Molly (Nikki's BFF), just in case she doesn't remember who I am. After I hand it back to her, Ethel inspects it and looks around the bar as though we just did a drug deal.

I'm about to slide out of the booth and get out of here when Midge walks into the bar and spots them, scowling at our table.

"There you two are. You're lucky I'm not dead. Some dog jumped at the car when he saw me and almost gave me a heart attack."

A tall guy comes in behind her and looks over. "Grandma, you cannot leave people asleep in the car."

He's cute, but I catch his wedding ring on his left ring finger. Of course he's taken.

"Pipe down, Austin." Dori slides out of the booth.

"I was taking Myles for a walk, and he recognized the Cadillac…" He nods outside where I assume he must've left the dog tied up.

The grandson—Austin, I guess—continues talking, but I don't think any of the women are paying attention to him.

"Our work here is done. Come on, Midge," Ethel says.

Dori and her grandson walk out, him lecturing her about being at a bar so late at night and the responsibility of being a good friend, while Ethel and Midge follow behind with me coming up the rear. Weirdest night ever.

———

I pull into the driveway of my house to find my mom's car plus another one parked along the side. After I've turned off the engine, I take in the place I've lived my entire life. It's a little worse for wear, paint chipping off the front porch and old windows. My mom always carries on about how this house was supposed to be a starter home, but then my dad up and left us, and she's barely been able to afford it since.

I climb out of my car and see the glow of a bonfire out back and hear my mother's laugh ringing through the air. A deep voice sounds next, apparently telling her some story that has her in hysterics. Not wanting to meet one of my mom's "friends," I opt to use the front door and make myself scarce.

Sliding off my shoes, I slowly turn the doorknob, unsurprised to find it unlocked. Our house is far enough back from the main road that no one ever comes here. I head to my bedroom and shut the door.

I flop back on my mattress and stare at the ceiling in need of a fresh coat of paint. I hate to admit that I might've been using Jed a little too. It was nice not to have to come home every night. Not to have to hear my mom's flirting, the headboard knocking on the wall, the moans from my mother's room. Not to deal with running into one of her "friends" in the bathroom.

But I can't escape this life until I can afford to move out on my own, which means I have to have enough to pay both our mortgage or rents, or at least chip in for hers.

People wonder why I embraced the reputation that I was easy. In some ways, it was just easier than trying to argue that some douchebag had made the whole thing up. Besides, it's what people expected from me when my mother was all over town, sleeping with any man who showed her the slightest bit of interest. Tourist season is always the worst.

I've seen more than one wedding ring tan line on the men she brings home, which is why I don't believe in monogamy. Would I actually trust a guy if he said he was going on a guys' trip? Absolutely not.

As I psychoanalyze myself, I realize that maybe that's why I go after guys like Jed. Guys who aren't looking for anything serious. I could've easily crushed on Cade or Xavier over the years. Both good guys who want a wife and a family. But it's always the bad boys who garner my attention.

I take my pillow, cover my face with it, and groan. Is this always going to be my life?

Hell no. It is not. I might never find a man deserving of me, one who can handle the baggage strapped to my back, but I can live for my career. Live for those little kids who need help. I want to see them succeed and trump the cards they were dealt.

With renewed confidence, I pull out my laptop and compose an email to Professor Locklear, telling him I have a lead on someone and that I don't know the specifics yet, but I'll fill him in as soon as I meet with him or her.

The squeak of a door from downstairs sounds and my mom continues to laugh, as though whoever she's with is a comedian who travels all over the world entertaining people. I'm surprised when the stairs don't creak and I don't hear my mom loudly shushing the man.

I listen at my door, straining to hear anything. There's nothing until a car engine roars to life and a car pulls out of the driveway. I watch the car and don't think I see a shadow in the passenger seat, so I head downstairs to grab something to eat and see if my mom is even still here.

I'm surprised to find her on the couch with the remote in her hand.

"I thought I saw your car out there." She glances at me and sets down the remote when she sees me turn into the kitchen. "I wish I'd known you were here. I wanted you to meet Troy."

"Sorry, I had to email my professor." See? I'm not even lying. "He's gone so soon?"

"He has to get on the boat tomorrow morning."

I roll my eyes and stare into the fridge. Another married guy with nothing to do while he's on land but screw people who aren't his wife. "Oh."

"He'll be gone for two weeks."

I grab a yogurt and shut the fridge. I don't say anything because anything I would say would be offensive.

"He works on one of the Bakers' boats."

My hand stops mid grab for a spoon. "He's from here?"

"Just returned actually. We went to high school together. He and your dad were—"

"Seriously?" I grab a spoon and slam the drawer shut with my hip.

"They were good friends, but none of that matters. He hasn't talked to your dad in longer than we have. He's out of both of our lives."

I nod and roll back on my heels.

"Anyway, when he returns, I'd like you to please come to dinner with us."

"Why?" I ask over a mouthful of yogurt.

"Because he asked me to marry him."

My eyes widen and land on the sizable diamond on her left ring finger. The yogurt slips from my hands, the spoon following right after, crashing to the floor.

Chapter Sixteen

Jed

Not wanting to be like every other dad, I decide not to take Emilia to the zoo, but rather to a glacier. She might as well see what it's like to live in Alaska sooner rather than later.

We drive up to Portage Glacier. From here, we can stop somewhere to eat and maybe hit a store. Hike a trail or something.

My heart races as we grow closer. This will be the first time it's just her and me having to converse for an entire day. Even if she doesn't say a lot yet.

After I park, I unbuckle her. Since she knows the drill now, she holds her hands up for me to pull her out. We've kind of mastered this nonverbal communication. Holding her in my arms, I lock the truck and head down the way to the ferry that will take us to see the glacier.

I watch Emilia while she looks around, soaking in her surroundings with wide eyes. I hand the tickets over and we climb aboard the boat. Emilia points at a flag flapping in the breeze, excitement overtaking her face. I smile and nod, confirming it's a flag.

By the time the boat leaves the dock, I'm surprised that it's only half filled. I would've thought there'd be more tourists wanting to see the glacier. I situate us toward the front of the boat. Emilia sits next to me, her hand on my thigh. She clenches it when the boat starts with a jerk that jolts both of our bodies. I hold her small hand, feeling her warmth. She squeezes it tightly when the boat jolts again before coasting through the water.

"It's okay. It's supposed to do that."

My reassurance earns no reaction. She barely looks at me and I don't blame her. I haven't been the one providing her comfort since she got here.

Her gaze is on the front of the boat, the water, and the mountain we're headed toward.

One of the tour guides comes over and squats so she can see Emilia's face. The woman is roughly my age, and she smiles at me as though she admires me having my daughter here. But she has no clue this is the first thing I've done for her.

"That's Portage Glacier," she says to Emilia, who nods. "We have to go by boat because it's been receding for centuries. There's a chance we might see the glacier calving, which is when a piece breaks off and goes into the water. It's pretty cool to watch." She looks at me when she says that, then she stands and takes the microphone from the stand and introduces herself as Avery to everyone else on the boat.

Avery talks into the microphone while the boat continues toward the glacier. She talks about the rock formations and why they look the way they do. When we sail by a waterfall, Emilia gets on her knees to look over the edge of the boat, resting her arms along the metal railing.

"Pretty cool, huh?" I ask, swiveling in my seat and placing one hand on her back.

Emilia nods and points at a bird soaring past, her mouth falling open a little.

I watch her intently as she takes in the beauty Alaska

has to offer. Her eyes widen as the boat rocks, and she points out the things Avery is talking about to the group. She's smart. I wish she'd speak to me.

Once we reach the glacier, I pick her up since the swarm of people are heading to the side of the boat that's closest. She again points at the glacier.

Avery surprises me when she starts talking right behind us. "The bluer the ice is, the more condensed it is."

I turn to find Avery's face inches away from mine and Emilia's. "Oh, cool."

"Yeah, it stretches six miles long."

I nod and smile as a thank you. "What do you think, little one?"

Emilia's lips tip up a little bit.

I'm growing a tad annoyed with Avery's presence. I'll give her a tip. She doesn't need to be hovering behind us.

The loud bang of cracking ice sounds out and Avery grabs the microphone. She describes the calving of the glacier with the excitement of a game show host. Thank goodness it's not a giant piece or that would spell trouble for this boat.

The piece falls off and everyone ohs and ahs. Even Emilia's mouth is slightly ajar. I watch her more than I do what's happening. Her gaze meets mine with amazement for a moment before returning to the scene in front of her.

Something in that moment captures me. We've shared this moment of excitement, and although she may never remember it, I'll remember it as the first time I felt that pull I should have when I first laid eyes on her. That pull that says she's mine, a piece of me.

I'm basking in the glow of really feeling like a father for the first time when she grips herself between her legs. As the boat rocks from the small ripples the glacier chunk caused, warm liquid trails down my arm and the side of my stomach.

"Emilia," I say, staring down at where she's obviously wet herself.

Her lower lip trembles and she cries.

"It's okay." I rub her back and walk over to Avery to see if she can direct me to a bathroom.

I'm informed there is no bathroom on the boat, but we'll be heading back in a little bit.

"Fuck," I murmur, then look at my daughter. "Don't repeat that. That's a bad word."

Her breath hitches as tears spill down her face, so I take her to the back of the boat where it's mostly vacant. Placing her feet on the ground, I inspect exactly what we're dealing with and find her jeans soaked. There's nothing I can do. I have no change of clothes. We probably should've used the bathroom before we got on the boat. Lesson learned.

I don't think this is a regular thing for her, but I realize that I really have no idea. Beyond that I have no idea about her medical history either since Tanya's passed away. I make a note to self to contact Dr. Bailey's office to get Emilia in for a checkup.

After we disembark from the boat, I head immediately to the truck and strap her in with my sweatshirt underneath her. I have no idea how I'm supposed to clean the car seat if it gets soiled, so I'm trying to prevent that. Emilia has calmed down, but she's still upset, staring down as though she did something wrong.

"This happens all the time." I give her shoulder a gentle squeeze.

Nothing.

"Your aunt Posey peed her pants all the time, and Aunt Nikki wet her bed until she was nine."

Nothing.

"It's okay, Emilia. You don't have to feel bad."

Nothing.

On the drive back to Sunrise Bay, I pull over at a tourist shop I doubt has any clothes for her, but at the very least I can get something to cheer her up. I do not want to drive for the next hour seeing her pouty lips in the rearview mirror.

I take her out of the car seat, figuring I already have pee all over me, so who cares? I walk into the small country store that has touristy items—magnets, pictures, shirts, mugs, and stuffed animals.

I set her down so she can look at the stuffed animals, then I glance through the children's clothing section. Luck is not on my side. Not one thing for her to wear on the bottom.

She tugs at my leg and hugs a stuffed puffin to her chest.

"Oh, the state bird," the woman who works there says. "Good choice. Did you see the baby puffin?"

"Do you have any children's pants?" I eye Emilia.

The woman shakes her head. She looks like a grandma, surely she'll help me out on this one.

"We don't. But we have a baby puffin." She picks up the stuffed animal and wiggles it in front of Emilia, who snatches it up and hugs it to the big puffin.

"Mama," she says so softly I can barely hear it.

"Yes, this is the mama and the baby," the woman says.

Emilia's smile dims and she hands the woman the big puffin.

The woman tries to hand it back to her. "Mama stays with her baby."

Emilia shakes her head and hands it back. My chest constricts painfully while the confused woman looks to me for an explanation, but I can't give her one right now. I want to break down with what's happening right now.

Emilia looks over the row of stuffed animals and picks up a moose, holding the baby puffin with the moose.

The woman's head tilts, and she studies Emilia for a moment. "The moose is a good choice too. You could get all three. Mommy." She holds out the big puffin. "Daddy." She points at the moose. "And you." She touches the baby puffin.

Emilia shakes her head. "No Mama," she says and walks away with just the moose and the baby puffin.

The woman stares at me, and I watch as Emilia stops to look at a row of books.

"Her mom passed away," I say.

The woman clutches the big puffin and her shoulders sink. Yeah, I figured that would be her response. Maybe next time she won't be so pushy. "Moms are never far away. I'll give you this one on the house. Maybe when she's ready."

"That's not necessary, I'll pay for it."

And now I feel like more of a shit dad because my daughter is clearly mourning her mother and I've been a jackass.

The woman rings me up and I throw in a candy bar to hopefully make Emilia smile.

We leave the store and I strap Emilia in, taking off her jeans so she's more comfortable for the rest of the ride home.

She eventually falls asleep in the truck, and I make a promise to myself that I'm going to figure this out. I'm going to get through to her, earn her trust, because I'm her father, her protector, and the one she'll rely on the most in this life.

I smile, seeing the moose and the baby puffin wrapped

in her small arms, then I glance at the big puffin in a bag next to me. I'm going to have to find a way to forgive Tanya for never telling me about Emilia. She was Emilia's mother, and no matter what my feelings are, that's the most important thing for me to remember.

Chapter Seventeen

Molly

A text comes from who I assume is Ethel a few days later.

Come to Northern Lights Retirement at four p.m.

I respond that I'll be there after I finish my shift at Truth or Dare. The bar isn't that busy because it's so sunny and warm outside, so everyone is enjoying it rather than being holed up at our place.

Cade comes behind the bar from the kitchen, a handful of papers in his hand. "How's it going?"

"It's slowish, so I expect you might be busy tonight." I cringe since I won't be able to stay late.

"It's fine. Xavier's helping out again."

"Don't you find that weird?" I fill my soda glass and sit on the stool behind the bar.

He shrugs. "Why is it weird?"

"Because usually in his off-season, he and Clara spend every waking moment together. But I've rarely seen the two of them together this summer. And now he wants to work at the bar? The man isn't exactly hard up for money."

"Good point. Maybe I should ask him about Clara." Cade does his usual thinking motion of pursed lips.

"It's up to you, but knowing you Greenes, it probably has to do with the fact that you're all twisted up inside."

He drops the papers on the bar and sets his gaze on mine. "Okay, I've gotta say it. What's the deal?"

I sip my soda and divert my gaze from Cade.

"Molly…"

"What?" I bite my lip.

"Please tell me nothing is going on with you and Jed?"

Did Fisher say something to him? Why would he think that? "Nothing's going on with me and Jed." And that's the truth—at least, now it is.

"You sure your Greene comment wasn't about Jed?"

I throw off the accusation. "No. Look at you with Presley. And Adam with Lucy. And now Xavier with Clara. Who's next?"

There are only a few Greene men left. Fisher, who is about as marriable as a priest. And Jed.

"Well, I don't think we're the only ones with issues." He eyes the door, and as I turn, I spot my mom walking in. "Ms. Monroe." He nods and smiles at her.

"Touché," I mumble and approach the section of the bar where my mom is headed.

"Hi, Cade, and I'm happy to report that I'll soon be a Mrs." She holds up her left hand.

I pour the usual beer she drinks and set it on the bar in front of her. I still can't believe she's getting married.

"Who's the lucky guy?" Cade eyes me as she sets her bags on the stool next to her.

"He's a fisherman. Works for the Bakers."

"Well, congratulations." He swings his arm around my shoulders. "Looks like you're going to be a stepdaughter now."

I wiggle out of his hold and shoot him a glare.

"I really should finish this paperwork up before dinner rush." Cade leaves after a few words with a local at the end of the bar.

My mom sips her beer. "Thanks."

I wait for her to tell me why she's here. This isn't my mom's usual haunt. She tends to hang out at the bars toward the city limits. That's what happens when you've been through most of the men in town.

"I'm off in a little bit." I eye the clock above the cash register.

Her eyes light up. "Great, then maybe we can do some shopping."

My mom and I do not do mother-daughter things like shop together. Actually, we've never really done much of anything together.

"Sorry, I have plans after work."

Her smile dims. "Oh."

I shouldn't feel guilty that now that she has time for me, she expects me to drop all my plans. "It's something for school. So I can graduate."

She nods and sips her drink. "Maybe you could pencil me into your busy life at some point."

I huff. "You could never find time to pencil me into yours."

"Molly," she sighs.

I raise my hand. "It's fine. I don't want to get into it with you. I have way too much on my plate right now."

A customer approaches the bar, so I go over to help him. And then I keep myself busy until Mom drops a twenty on the bar top and leaves with a quick goodbye and a wave.

Once she's gone, I watch her walk past the window before I take her glass and the money, wiping her area clean. Troy must do well and leave her money to spend if she left me a twenty. Guilt gnaws at me, but I'm not sure what she expects when she left me to fend for myself my entire life.

Xavier comes in fifteen minutes later, his usual smile and easygoing attitude absent today. Sure, I could ask what's bugging him, but I'm not getting involved in any more of the Greenes' business except for Nikki, and technically she's not even a Greene anymore.

I clock out and use my hip to jut the back door open, finding Jed on the other side with a case of beer in his hands. The mere sight of him brings my anger from how he acted at the summer bash to the surface. Still, I use my foot to keep the door open for him.

"Thanks," he mumbles, his eyes trained on the box of beer.

"It's okay, Jed, you can look at me. My eyes aren't all red-rimmed from heartbreak."

He looks up at me. "I'm sor—"

"Shove your sorry up your ass, Jed!" I walk to my car.

Seriously? Does he really think I'm crushed because whatever we had was over? It's over because I said it was over.

Still, as the metal door slams shut, a piece of my heart shocks that he just went on with what he was doing and didn't try to stop me to talk to him. Only confirming I don't mean a whole helluva lot to him.

*N*orthern Lights Retirement Home screams money. The outside of the huge estate is a luscious green this time of year, and the gardens are full of annuals that are bursting with color. It reminds me of a country club, not that I've ever been to one. Sometimes I wonder why elderly people want to live in Alaska for their remaining days. I mean, I love Alaska, but they can't enjoy all it offers. I can't picture Dori and Ethel skiing down a hill or hiking through the woods without breaking something.

I park my car, which looks like a junker compared to the other ones in the parking lot, and spot Dori's Cadillac in one of the many handicapped spots. Walking down the pathway, I continue under the overhang and through the front door. A giant bouquet of flowers sits on a polished round table under a chandelier in the foyer. Like I said, money. And it makes me itch.

"Hi, I'm here to see Ethel Greene," I tell the woman behind the desk.

She looks up. "Granddaughter?"

"Friend." I smile.

"Between her, Dori, and Midge, I can never keep track of who is who and which family they're from. You don't have to check in with me. This isn't a hotel. Do you know which way to go?" She stands as though she's going to direct me, but Midge walks by.

"Bar girl," she says to me and pushes up her black-rimmed glasses. Her blouse is askew and she looks as if she just worked out, but not in the fitness room.

"Hi, Midge."

"I'll take her to Ethel. I saw that little girl with her before I went to Earl's room."

I'm not sure who the little girl or Earl is, but it's clear to me that I was probably right about what Midge was just up to.

"Thanks for your help." I smile at the woman behind the desk, who inhales deeply, looking Midge up and down. She seems like she wants to say something but refrains.

Although I don't want to picture it, I think it's pretty awesome that Midge is still getting it on at her age.

I walk with her down a hallway.

"Earl has narcolepsy, so these are his peak hours." Midge elbows me and smiles.

"Oh, that's good." What am I supposed to say? Should I high-five her and congratulate her for the score like we're a bunch of football players in high school?

"Ethel and Dori swear they're never going to get married again. I always tell them, you don't have to marry 'em to sleep with 'em. Be more progressive."

"I couldn't agree more."

"Then I'd watch out." Her hand lands on my forearm and she stops us. "Be careful. Those two are notorious for trapping their grandchildren."

"Oh, I'm not one of their grandchildren." I pat her hand. She must be confused.

"I know, dear. My glasses might be thick, but I'm not blind."

Oops. I didn't mean to insult her. "Sorry."

"But—"

"Molly!" Ethel yells from two doors down. "What are you talking about, Midge?"

Ethel eyes Midge as if she's a Mafia boss and if Midge doesn't keep her secrets, she'll be sleeping with the fishes. And there are a lot of places for that in Alaska.

"Nothing. I was coming back from Earl's."

Ethel eyes her. "I can see that. Straighten out your blouse. I hope you're using condoms."

Midge waves her off. "Don't worry about me."

"You're not too old to get an STD!" she yells after Midge before ushering me toward her apartment.

"Thank you, Midge," I say, but she only lifts her arm halfway up in a wave.

"Thank you for coming here. It's so much easier for me that way, you know?" Ethel waves her hand over and over until I step inside her apartment. Then she shuts and locks the door. Weird, but I'm pretty sure I can take her if I need to.

I turn to find Emilia sitting on the couch with a book in her lap. I still, not expecting to find the child of the man I just stopped sleeping with here for me to help.

"I was just helping her a little bit," Ethel says. "We were going over the family members. Primarily me."

"Jed dropped her here before he went to work?" I ask.

Ethel gets a weird look on her face.

"I just saw him when I left."

Her nostrils flare. "Really?"

I nod, wondering why Jed wouldn't have said something to me about this. Of course, I didn't give him much of a chance.

"Okay, well, let's get started." Ethel walks toward the couch. "Emilia, this is Molly!" She enunciates each word and speaks louder than she does to her peers.

Emilia waves at me.

I sit on the couch and look at the book. Right now, it's on a family photo with a bunch of people in it. If Ethel thinks Emilia's going to learn all these names, she's wrong. I pull a book about animals and what their fur or skin feels like from the pile.

"We're good," I tell Ethel, because Emilia keeps glancing between her and me.

"Okay, I'll be in my bedroom."

Ethel walks away, and thankfully, she shuts the door. I really don't want her hovering over us the whole time.

"Can I ask you a question, Emilia, and can you try to answer me with one word?"

She nods.

"How old are you?"

She puts up her hand with three fingers out.

"Can you say it?"

"Three," she says quietly.

"That's a great age. Thank you for using your voice."

My suspicion is that while Emilia's vocabulary may be limited, she's not talking because she doesn't feel comfortable talking. The trauma she's been through is tremendous and we're still all strangers to her at this point.

"Do you know which animal this is?" I point at a page in the book.

"Quack."

"And how does the fur feel?"

She runs her hand over the yellow faux fur. She wraps her arms around her torso, giving herself a hug.

"Soft?" I ask.

She nods.

"Can you repeat after me and say soft?"

"Ofd," she says.

"That's good. Okay, let's keep going." I turn the page.

The further we get, the more comfortable she becomes. The tension in her facial expressions eases and she laughs at some of the things I say or I do. She's the cutest kid ever.

Forty-five minutes or so later, we're on the floor, working on a small puzzle.

"What did you do yesterday?" I ask.

Her eyes widen and she goes to the couch, grabbing a small stuffed puffin and moose. She holds them out for me.

"Did you get these?" I ask.

She nods.

"Can you say yes?"

"Yes," she says well.

"Where did you get them?"

Her arms go to her side. "Whoosh." Both her hands go down.

I'm not quite sure what she's telling me. "Did something fall?"

She nods.

A knock on the door startles us both, and she sits down, nudging closer to me.

I place my hand on her back. "No worries. I'll get it."

I stand and head toward the door, but Ethel's bedroom door opens first. Man, she's speedy when she wants to be.

"I got it," she says.

"Bibi!" Jed says from the other side. "You guys in there?" Another knock.

I look back at Emilia, who seems more relaxed now and is looking at the animal puzzle pieces, trying to fit one in a spot it doesn't go.

"Um… give me a second," Ethel says.

"Ethel?" I ask.

Another knock.

"Jed, this is a retirement community," Dori's voice sounds on the other side of the door.

"Just open the door," I say to Ethel.

"Dori, I don't need your antics right now. I just want to grab Emilia." The authority in Jed's voice is nice to hear. Like he's claimed her as his daughter now. "Open the door, Bibi!"

I round Ethel and unlock and open the door.

Jed freezes for a moment, then crosses the threshold. "What the hell is going on here?"

You'd think from his reaction, he just found Emilia next to a pound of cocaine and a scale.

Chapter Eighteen

"My child isn't for sale."
— Jed

Jed

"Just relax," Molly says, putting her hand on my chest while I feel like storming the room.

"Molly is right," Bibi says. "This was a good thing."

I look at Emilia, who is busy with a puzzle, but I see the books strewn about. I'm not as dumb as people think I am. I know what this is.

"You went behind my back to give her speech therapy?" I eye Molly.

Molly looks at Bibi and Dori.

"You know what…" Dori walks gingerly across the room, takes Emilia's hand, and leads her toward the door.

I put my hand on Emilia's other one. "Oh, no, you don't. She stays."

"We have ice cream in the cafeteria," Dori says, which garners Emilia's attention.

Emilia tugs her hand out of mine.

"You're ditching me for some vanilla ice cream?" I look down at her. I've felt a kinship with her since our excursion.

"We have chocolate ice cream too," Dori says.

My gaze shifts up to her and I tilt my head. "Are you trying to kidnap her?"

"Jed, stop it." Bibi smacks my hand as if I'm five.

"You're the only one I can trust in this room besides Emilia. Tell me what's going on?" I say to Molly, who is across the room, collecting her stuff.

"What do you want me to say? I didn't know you weren't aware."

I can't tell if she's lying. "Wouldn't I have said something to you an hour ago at Truth or Dare if I'd known?"

She drops her bag. "Oh yeah, because you were so talkative." Molly is the queen of attitude. "If you have an issue, take it up with your grandma."

"She's my grandma, not Emilia's mother!" I yell.

The door slams shut, and I look to my left to see that Emilia, Dori, and Bibi are all gone. I turn around and place my hand on the doorknob, but when I pull, nothing happens.

"Bibi! Dori!" I yell, pounding my fist on the door.

"You're going to give someone a heart attack. This isn't the place for that." Molly comes to my side, hitting me with her hip to get me out of the way, and tries the doorknob.

I cross my arms. "Do you think you're stronger than me?"

She balks. "Of course, you're all, 'I'm man, man stronger than woman.'" She lowers her voice to a gruff-sounding male one.

I scowl at her. "What are you even talking about?"

She turns the knob and pulls.

Nothing.

"How are those muscles working for you?" I lean against the wall.

"Why would they lock us in and how on earth did they even do that?" Molly stares at the door as though she has the ability to see through it.

"If you hadn't been hiding this from me, then we wouldn't be in this predicament."

She points at herself. "You're blaming me? You're fucking crazy."

"No need for cursing." I'm the one pointing at her now. "You're secretly giving therapy to my daughter."

She shakes her head. "And if I were, what is the problem with that? Because she needs it, if you didn't notice. She went through something traumatic and needs to trust someone."

"And that person should be you?" I drop my hands to my sides and clench my fists.

She narrows her eyes at me. "Do you think this is my way of getting to you?"

I shrug, and she scoffs. Truth is, I didn't really think that until she said it, but girls have been known to go further in their pursuits before.

"Oh. My. God!" she screeches. "How arrogant can you be? Let me fill you in on something Jed Greene." God, her tits look good in that Truth or Dare shirt.

I shake my head. Stay on task. "It's not arrogance."

"I could strip right here, and you'd fuck me on that couch. Hell, you'd fuck me against the wall, and we both know it. You need to remember who ended this."

Now I scoff. "Because you wanted dinners and shit."

She laughs manically and twirls around as if she can't stand the sight of me. "Dinners and shit? How about some respect? How about not wanting to be used?"

Her words are like a blow to my chest. I open my mouth and shut it, still processing what she just said.

She shakes her head. "Forget what I said."

"Molly," I say, unsure what else to say.

"I said forget it," she snaps.

I stand there silently. *Say something, anything.* "Well,

regardless of what happened between us, you can't go behind my back with my daughter."

She glances over her shoulder, and if glares could kill you, I'd be on the ground clutching my chest right now.

"I'm dealing with Emilia," I say.

She circles and gives me her full-on glare. It's kind of scary. "Really? Because from where I'm standing, it looks like you're doing the complete opposite."

"I'm trying, okay? And I don't need advice from you. You have no idea what this is doing to me."

She scoffs. "Actually, I do, because I know you pretty well. But she's your daughter. Your flesh and blood. And so what if I'm helping her? What's the harm if I can help her communicate verbally with you, with her new family?"

Stubborn to a fault and not wanting to admit she has a point, I walk over to Bibi's fridge, needing something to drink. But unless I want every type of juice known to man, that's not going to happen.

"Stop changing the subject. Why are you so pissed that Ethel asked me to help her?" Molly walks toward me.

"Don't worry about it." I go over to the front door and try again. Still locked.

"You're just going to run away again?"

I swivel and she's there, then steps away, her eyes blazing with a fury that makes me want to kiss her senseless. "I'm not running. Remember, you ended this, so I'm not really your concern anymore. Which means neither is Emilia."

She shakes her head in disgust. "Don't act like you ever really let me in. You keep everyone at arm's length."

"You don't know what you're talking about." I knock on the door, hoping someone will hear and let me out of here.

"So you had a shitty dad. You don't have a monopoly

on daddy issues, Jed. I never had a dad. He didn't even want me."

I squeeze my eyes shut, not wanting to get into this.

"He didn't try to buy my love with new trucks and quarterback positions. He just didn't want me, and as a result, my mom buried herself in men to try to forget him. So maybe that's why I'm here helping Emilia… because I know what it's like to not be number one in my parents' life."

Her words cut me as deep as I'm sure she meant them to.

"I'm saving her," I whisper. "Saving her from disappointment."

"How about you just don't disappoint her?"

Her question is valid. It's one I've asked myself a million times already—am I capable of not disappointing my daughter in the long run?

I whip around to face her again. "Goddamn it, Molly, just stay the fuck out of it."

"Just keep adding those bricks to the wall," she says.

Anger overwhelms me because she's scratching away at my deepest scar. "You want to talk about bricks? All right, I'm game. Tell me why you hide yourself in men?"

She balks and steps back, her mouth open.

"You know exactly what I'm talking about. Offering yourself up to every douchebag who sniffs around. Like you want to prove that asshole from high school right."

She shakes her head. "You're crossing a line you know nothing about."

I cross my arms and widen my stance. "You're putting your two cents in on my life. I think it's only fair we examine yours."

She pulls out her cell phone. "I'm calling the police to get us out of here."

"Can't stand the heat, huh? Dish it out, but you can't take it?"

Her fingers fly across the screen of her phone. "What are you, twelve?"

"Just answer me. Why do you do it?"

"It's none of your business." She stabs at the screen some more. "Ugh, what did they do, tear down the cell phone tower?" She pockets her cell phone. "I'm going to climb out the window."

"Come on, Molly, I thought we were having a conversation." I continue to egg her on when I know I should let this go. She's obviously flustered. "Why did you let me fuck you without the promise of even a dinner?"

Her chest rises and falls with a deep breath. "It's not the same with you as it is with the others."

"What does that mean?" I step forward.

"Nothing."

"Come on. Tell me."

She rolls her eyes. "Why? You need the ego boost? Please."

I stare at her for a long moment. "Tell me."

She fixes her gaze on mine. "My freshman year, your senior year. The kiss behind the concession stand."

I smile, remembering. At the time, I didn't know she'd end up being my sister's best friend. "I remember."

"And do you remember telling me you'd find me after? And then do you remember going off with Lila Turner when the game was done?"

I step back and close my eyes. "I did that to help you. I was an asshole in high school, especially when I first moved here. All the guys were already talking about that bullshit Matty was spewing and I knew I didn't want anything serious with anyone, so I figured it was better to save you from having to deal with the rumors that would've started if we'd been seen together."

My mind was still fucked up from my parents' divorce, my dad cheating on my mom. I liked Molly, but I barely knew her.

"I hurt you," I say, realizing for the first time that my actions had the opposite effect I'd intended. I thought she'd just think I was an asshole and forget the whole thing.

She shakes her head. "No." Her tone is definitive, but I hear the tinge of sadness in it, and I see the tears welling in her eyes. She puts her arms out to her sides. "I'm the town slut. How could you hurt me?"

"No, you're not," I say vehemently. "Although I never understood why you undervalued yourself."

A tear slips down her face, but she quickly wipes it away. "Let's just forget this. You don't want me to help Emilia, I won't. End of."

I should take her deal. Keep my mouth shut and sit here in silence until the two crazy grandmas finally let us out. But I need to make this right. "I wasn't using you. Not really."

She shakes her head, staring at her feet while she wipes away her tears. "It's over. Doesn't matter anymore."

"No. I just… I thought we were on the same page. Yes, at first I was probably a prick, ignoring my problems with the distraction of you. That wasn't fair." I move forward hesitantly because Molly could kick me in the nuts. "But it wasn't like you were interchangeable and it could've been anyone in your place."

"Just stop. I don't want to talk about it." She turns around to face the wall, and I use the opportunity to move closer to her.

"You should know that I couldn't get enough of you. I never would've thought that the first time wouldn't be enough. I craved you when you weren't in my bed. Late at night, I still think about how soft you felt pressed to me." I put my hands on her hips. "I'm sorry I hurt you. Back in high school and in the last few weeks. Truly, I am." Her back racks up and down with rapid breaths. "Turn around."

She slowly circles in my arms. My gaze dips to her lips. How easy it would be to end this fight between us with one press of my lips to hers. I bet the make-up sex would be out of this world.

"Fine. You're forgiven," she mumbles.

I tilt my head because her tone isn't convincing.

"It's fine. Honestly. I was on board. It's not all on you. I mean, the high school thing is." A non-genuine laugh escapes her. "But not the most recent stuff."

"Molly, you have my word that if I ever come on to you again, it'll be because I want more than a fling, okay?" I can tell by her expression that she won't be holding her breath and waiting for that day to come. I don't blame her. "So is this a truce?"

"Go back to who we were before?" Her forehead wrinkles.

I shake my head. "No."

"I can't do this." She waves a finger between us. "I can't be your booty call. I'm sorry."

"Friends. We can be friends." Every part of me wants to pull her flush to me. I want to kiss her and hold her, but I need to push those feelings away. I can't keep being so reckless with people's feelings, and that starts with Emilia and Molly.

"Okay." She nods.

I rest my forehead on hers again and we both inhale a deep breath.

Noise from the other side of the door tears us away

from one another. Then the door opens and Bibi pops her head in.

"That silly Earl put a chair under the door. You guys okay?"

Emilia has chocolate ice cream all over her face, but she's smiling. That brings a smile to my face.

"Cute, Bibi," I say, picking up Emilia and taking her over to the sink. "Earl isn't the culprit."

"If Midge was with Earl before I got here, then I'm sure he's napping. Cut the act." Molly picks up her bag. "Bye, Emilia." She waves. "Jed."

With a nod, Molly is out the door. I somehow stop myself from following her.

"Next time you want to watch Emilia, the answer is no if you're going to hide things from me," I say.

Bibi acts offended with her hand over her heart. "What? Molly needs to find a child."

I shake my head. "I don't even understand what that means, and besides, my child isn't for sale." I pick Emilia up, grab her coat, and flee the retirement community.

Who knew a bunch of old people could cause so much trouble?

Chapter Nineteen

Jed

Something about the quietness of the brewery when I open it up by myself always brings me a sense of peace. Sometimes my mind wanders back to when this was just a dream for Cade and me, and how somehow we were able to pull it off without any help from our parents. We've even talked about expanding into Greywall if we can find a suitable building. I never would've thought that would be a possibility when we were starting out.

A knock on the front window drags me out of my thoughts. When I look up, Nikki's at the glass, scowling and obviously annoyed.

Great. This should be fun.

After walking through the brewery, I unlock and open the front door.

She barrels through without even a hello. "What is wrong with you?"

I lock the door behind her. "Well, hello to you too. How is the pregnancy going? Let me grab a case of beer for poor Logan."

She tosses her bag on a table and puts both hands on her hips. Her belly is even bigger than the last time I saw her. "Funny. You know, I get that you can be an asshole. I mean, you like to do what you like and blah, blah, blah, but you'd think you'd help your daughter. How cold can you be?"

I continue rolling the cutlery. I need to get into the stills, but with Nikki here, it will have to wait. "What are you talking about?"

"Grandma Ethel's? Yesterday? You going crazy over Molly helping Emilia? She *is* about to graduate with her degree in speech pathology, you know."

I stop and put both palms on the table. "They never okayed it with me."

"Because you've been blind to everything that's going on. I know they can overstep, but it's good for Emilia. Besides, Molly didn't even know it was Emilia she was going to be helping when she was told to show up there. And Grandma Ethel said that they were making progress. If you won't do it because it's good for Emilia, why can't you just do it for Molly's sake?"

I shake my head, trying to catch up to what she's saying. "What the hell are you talking about? What does Molly get from this?"

She blows out a breath. "Like you don't know."

"I don't."

"Her degree. The family she was doing her clinical with left her high and dry, and now she won't graduate until she finds another kid to help. I mean, I get that Dad was always like, 'hide your inadequacies,' but I thought we both agreed he's an asshole."

"Wait. She might not graduate?"

Another long, annoyed breath flows out of her mouth. "Yes. Are you listening to me?"

"I didn't know anything about that." Which is true. No one mentioned that to me. Hell, I was about to ask Molly to help me yesterday, but I didn't want to ask her for a favor after she thought I was using her. I made an appointment with a pediatrician first thing this morning to discuss things further but I can't get in until next week.

"What do you mean? Grandma Ethel said she told you all of this and you still said no."

I tilt my head and raise my eyebrows.

"Damn them." She walks across the room. "I need a water."

I beat her behind the bar and get her a glass. "Sit down and let's talk without you screaming at me."

She slides onto the same stool she's used ever since we opened. The one where she keeps Molly from working and Cade always complains about it. Thank god Molly was on board to remain friends after our fling, otherwise Nikki would probably be beating me with her purse. Who knows the moves Logan's showed her? She did marry a retired MMA fighter.

"I can't believe she tricked me. I was up all night fuming." Nikki sucks down half of the glass of water.

"We all know Dori's reputation, and Bibi's been trying to get every one of us matched up. We're not even her actual grandchildren. What does she care?"

She gives me a look. "She thinks of us as her own and we think of her as a grandma and you know it."

"Do you think she's pushing something here? Like, between Molly and me?" My heart beats out a staccato rhythm as I wonder how Nikki will react. She's always protected Molly. Last night in bed, when I was reflecting on my conversation with Molly, I remembered that the morning after I kissed Molly behind the concession stand, Nikki woke me up by hitting me in the face with a pillow and telling me never to touch Molly or talk to her again.

"I think they have some crazy plan, yes. They brought that Allie to Mom and Hank's to fix her up with you. I don't know why they're bringing Molly into the mix."

"Maybe she's just concerned about Emilia."

She huffs.

"Hey," I say.

Nikki puts up her hand. "I don't mean they don't want the best for Emilia and to get her to talk, but if that was all Grandma Ethel wanted, she wouldn't have had you pick Emilia up. She would have made sure Molly was gone well before you came. They aren't amateurs in coercion."

Nikki has a point. But they want to fix me up with Molly? That idea shouldn't make me smile, but it does. Because they have no idea we've already slept together. Do they see something I'm missing?

"What's with the smile?" Nikki asks.

I straighten my lips. "Nothing."

She sips more of her water. "You and Molly are way too similar to ever work out."

My forehead wrinkles. "What's that mean?"

"You know."

"Enlighten me."

"Neither of you want to get married. You're both all about no strings, one-night affairs. I mean, I think if a guy called Molly twice, she'd catch hives." Another sip of her water. I grab the glass when she's done with it.

"Coffee?" I turn as though I'm going to get some, but I just want to hide my reaction.

Picturing Molly with other guys isn't exactly pleasant. But I smile when I remember that she had no problem when I called her for thirds and fourths.

When I turn back, Nikki shakes her head. "Had my cup for today." She rubs her stomach as though the baby is a reminder that she can't have more. "I mean, I want Molly to be happy and I don't think she wants to be like her mother. Who, did you hear, is getting married?" She rolls her eyes. "But you're not the guy for Molly. I'm going to have to intercede. Be smarter than those old biddies."

"Why am I not good enough?" Irritation flares inside me.

"Do you have a notebook for me to write all the reasons down?" She must feel guilty after seeing my expression because she says, "Come on, you know you're not the settling down type. Plus, you have Emilia now. I'd say you've had enough change for the time being without having to try and be a doting boyfriend."

She gets up off the stool before I can say anything.

"Can we circle back to what Molly needs?" I ask.

Walking over to the table where she left her purse, Nikki swings it over her shoulder and smiles brightly at me. "She needs Emilia and you to agree to speech therapy with her. To be a case study so she can graduate."

"Done," I say, without thinking too much about it. If I do, I'll only talk myself out of it, and clearly this is what's best for my daughter and my friend.

"Really? Thanks so much! And I'm sorry about the whole yelling thing."

"It's okay, I'm used to everyone thinking the worst of me."

She's already walking away, but she circles back around to face me. "You know that's not true. You're a great guy. Your priorities are a little screwed up, but I think that little girl of yours might just turn you around." She grins and turns back to the door.

"But I'm not good enough for your best friend, huh?" I can't help myself.

She laughs and pauses with her hand on the door. "That's not an invitation to prove me wrong. Don't worry about Grandma Ethel and Dori, I'll figure out a way to detour them from their mission."

She's out the door and walking toward her podcast studio before I have time to say anything more.

After putting her glass in the washer, I head back to the barrels, wanting to check a cream ale I've been messing with. The best part of owning this brewery is making my own beers.

I push what Nikki said out of my head. Like she said, it's not a challenge. Deal with Emilia. Figure that out before I go thinking there might be something more with Molly.

---

*A*round lunchtime, Molly walks in the back door.

"Hey," I say, since I was headed to the kitchen.

"Hi." She walks into the staff changing area and I switch directions, following her in.

She senses me and looks over her shoulder, going to her locker. "What's up?"

"Nikki came to see me this morning," I tell her, sliding onto the bench.

"About what? She called me last night."

"And what did you tell her?"

She takes off her jacket, and there are those amazing tits in a Truth or Dare T-shirt like always. It's always slightly turned me on, but now that I've held them and felt the weight of them in my palms, my reaction is at another level. I've seen how hard her dusty nipples get. I know how much she loves when I play with them and suck them. *All right, pervert, get back on the subject of your daughter's therapy.*

"I didn't answer. She left a voice mail. I called her back this morning when I knew she was recording and left a message."

I nod. "She came in throwing a few accusations my

way. Why didn't you tell me about needing help to graduate yesterday?"

She stuffs her jacket in the locker, grabs a clean apron, and ties it around her waist. She truly is gorgeous, and I have no idea why I never noticed before. Her dark hair cascades down her face until she tucks it behind her ear. "Because it's not your problem."

"I'm your boss and your friend."

She glances up through her dark eyelashes and smirks at my friend reference. "Don't go saving me, Jed."

"I'm not, but Emilia does need help and I'd rather it be you than anyone else."

"You felt differently last night." She grabs a pen and pad before shutting and locking her locker.

"Because I don't like it when people do things behind my back. My dad did shit behind my back all the time when I was younger, and I don't like being in the dark when it concerns my own life." I try to keep my voice light even though talking about how my dad manipulated my life burns.

"What's changed? Nikki's temper?" She stands with her back to the locker, her hands tucked behind her.

I stand, knowing I should stay seated but unable to at this moment. "Please, Molly? Help Emilia communicate with words so I can build a relationship with her. Help my daughter."

She stares at me for a long moment. "You'd have to sign some papers. Agree to be a case study. I have to have videos of her."

I nod.

"This isn't going to be behind closed doors. Anything I suggest needs to be incorporated by everyone who watches her—Marla, Fisher, you, and whoever else. It's not just a me and Emilia thing."

"I'll do anything to help her. Name it."

She inhales and I do too, our eyes locked. "And whatever happened between us stays in the past. This is strictly me helping you and Emilia. No after-hours lessons for Daddy."

I almost wince at the word daddy, still absorbing the fact that I am one. I have a flirty response begging to be unleashed, but I bite my lip and swallow it. "Deal."

"Okay. I'll get everything going. How about I come by tomorrow? You can sign the papers and we'll get started."

"Sounds perfect," I say, clenching my fists so I don't put them above her on the locker and lean in.

She smiles and slides around me. "Great. I better clock in."

Before I blink, she's gone, and the door shuts quietly.

Damn, I need to get a grip. This is my little sister's best friend, my employee, and now my daughter's speech therapist.

Chapter Twenty

Molly

I head over to Jed's with a bin full of supplies, since I don't think Emilia has a ton of toys yet. I talked to Professor Locklear and he agreed that we need to get her to start talking before we make any definitive guesses as to whether she's behind. We discussed the trauma she's been through and how I need to become someone she can trust, that I need to make this a fun experience and not work.

The door opens before I have to knock, and Jed takes the bin from my arms.

"Oh, thanks." I shake out my arms. Between the books and puzzles, it was heavy. I'd never admit that to him, however.

"Thanks for coming," he says.

I smile and glance around the space I almost don't recognize. "Did you… clean?"

The mail bin has been cleaned out, and the Xbox controllers are tucked away instead of strewn wherever they left them when they were done playing. There are also no stray beer bottles or bags of chips lying around.

"I did. I told Emilia we had to make it nice. She helped me take the recycling out." He puts the bin on the floor next to the couch. "I'll go get her. She's in her bedroom."

"May I?" I point up the stairs. "Is her room where she feels the safest?"

He stops at the bottom of the stairs. "I think so. I mean, she likes to stay in there."

"Then that's a great place to start."

A smile tips his lips, and I'm struck once again by what a gorgeous man he is. How am I ever going to pull this off without my body yearning for his?

We walk up the stairs, and Jed knocks before opening the door. Emilia's on her bed with the stuffed baby puffin and moose, her ostrich sitting right behind them.

"Hey, Emilia," I say.

She smiles.

"I guess I'll leave you guys to it. Emilia, Molly's going to spend some time with you, but I'll be downstairs."

She nods.

"Thanks again," Jed says and leaves the room.

The door clicks shut, and I look around the room at all of Adam's stuff, the things he never took to his other house. The bed is a queen, and the bedspread is blue denim while the furniture is all brown. This is no room for a little girl. I had plans for the books and puzzles, but I think I have a much better idea.

"Do you like your room, Emilia?"

She shrugs.

"Can you tell me about your room before this one?"

"Pink," she says.

"Pink's a good color. Do you think you'd want this room to be pink?"

She shakes her head.

"Do you have a favorite color?"

She shakes her head again.

I pull out my phone and scroll to find a color wheel, but then I decide on something different. I've heard Jed talk about redoing Emilia's room anyway, and there's no time like the present.

"Do you want to go for a ride into town?" I ask, pocketing my cell phone. "Your dad will have to come with us."

She giggles at my scrunched-up nose.

"Let's go do some convincing." I wave her up, and she grabs the ostrich. "Is ostrich coming?"

She nods.

"Does your ostrich have a name?"

"Betty," she says so clearly that my heart leaps.

"Hi, Betty, I'm Molly." I pretend to shake hands with it.

Emilia laughs and tucks Betty under her arm. Her hand slides into mine and we descend the stairs, surprising Jed as he opens the pile of mail that sits in the center of the kitchen table.

"What are you two doing?" His gaze zeros in on where we're holding hands. "I see you two are getting along."

"We'd like to go to Handyman Haven," I say politely.

He pushes the chair back from the table. "Why?"

"It's a field trip. Live a little. Can you drive us?"

He gets up and abandons the mail. "You want to go to the hardware store?" he clarifies as though I'm crazy.

I look down at Emilia and we both smile. "Yes."

"For what?"

"Don't worry about it," I say in a teasing voice.

"Molly," he says with warning in his tone, but I roll my eyes and he stops insisting on knowing every detail right away.

The three of us leave the house and file into his truck. Instead of sitting up front with him, I sit in the back with Emilia.

"Why are you sitting back there?" he complains when starting the truck.

"Because I'm here for Emilia, not you." I look at Emilia and take her hand.

"I look like a damn chauffeur," he complains but continues to back out of the driveway. Unfortunately, it's kind of hot the way he has one hand around the back of the passenger seat and is turned and looking over his shoulder.

I shake my head at him. "Just relax."

He blows out a breath and drives without saying a word.

"Do you like music, Emilia?" I ask.

She nods.

"Do you have a favorite song?"

She shakes her head.

I tap my lips with my finger. "I've got a few. Jed, can you hook up my phone to your Bluetooth?"

He meets my gaze in the rearview mirror. "Just use mine." He hands me his phone without any qualms.

I shouldn't like the fact it's clear he's not hiding anything, but I do anyway.

I scroll through his music app, searching for what I'm looking for.

"You know you're going to ruin my entire 'for you' suggestions," he says with humor.

"Hate to break it to you, but these are going to be your new 'for you' suggestions anyway."

He chuckles. "You're probably right."

I press play on "Five Little Monkeys Jumping on the Bed," and when it starts, I put up my hand with five fingers and animate the song. Emilia is enthralled, watching me with wide eyes and a bright smile. I hold her hand up and manipulate her fingers to join me and continue bopping around and exaggerating all my expressions.

"She loves it," Jed mumbles, staring more at us in the rearview mirror than the road.

The song ends and I fall back into the seat and blow out a breath as though I'm exhausted. A few more kids' songs play until we pull into the downtown area. Jed parks in the lot behind Truth or Dare.

While he gets Emilia out of the truck, I get out on my side and meet them behind the truck.

"If speech therapy doesn't pan out, you have a career in child entertainment." Jed smiles and heads toward the back doors of Truth or Dare.

"Nope." I point for us to go around and enter the square on the side by the meat market.

"I thought we'd just stop in," he says.

"You're not working, and we're going to Handyman Haven."

He's holding Emilia's hand while I'm a little in front of them. I turn around and step backward.

He follows me. "Tell me why again?"

"You'll find out when we get there."

He grumbles something under his breath, but we walk through the opening by the meat market, waving to Chuck in the window. He's butchering a large piece of meat in his blood-stained apron.

"I'm not sure I understand why he thinks this is appealing," I say, and Jed laughs.

"He said he thinks it's akin to when candymakers show how they make taffy and stuff." He's obviously asked Chuck about it before.

"Someone needs to tell him it's not the same."

"Not in the slightest."

We both chuckle and Emilia laughs as though she understands us. Maybe she does.

As we walk up the cobblestone street, Emilia's small

hand slides into mine. I glance to my right, finding Jed watching intently. He's holding her other hand. His gaze shifts to mine and we hold our gazes for a moment.

"What are you guys doing?" A voice pulls our attention away from each other.

We both look forward at Presley, whose eyes are on our adjoined hands.

"We're headed to Handyman Haven," I say, and look down at Emilia. "Right?"

She nods a few times.

"And they're keeping it a secret from me as to the reason why," Jed says.

Presley's smile grows as she takes us in. "Sounds like fun."

She's clearly having thoughts about seeing us like this. We resemble a family, though we're not.

Presley crouches in front of Emilia. "And you need to come to story time at the bookstore soon. What's your favorite story?"

Emilia shrugs.

"You don't have one?" Presley acts surprised. "You need to come into my shop sometime and pick out a book. It's on me. Every little girl should have a favorite book." She touches Emilia's nose with her finger and stands back up.

"You know what? We'll come by right after we finish at Handyman Haven." I smile at Jed, who blows out a breath.

"You do know I have things to do today, right?" he says.

"I heard you have the day off," Presley says, narrowing her eyes at him.

"I do more than just work," Jed says.

"Stop complaining. Let's go. We'll see you in a bit, Presley."

We walk past her and she heads back toward the chalk-board outside her store, continuing to use chalk to decorate the board.

"Keep cracking the whip, Mol." She laughs.

"You can't crack the whip when my hand is still my best friend," Jed calls out.

"You can't talk like that in front of Emilia," I scold him, and he stops us.

"She has no idea what I'm saying. And anyway, tell me I'm wrong."

I tug us forward, Emilia dragging Jed with us. "You're not wrong, I guess."

All I can envision is his hand on his dick. Stroking and tugging and the way his face looks when he comes. The sounds he makes. Shaking my head, I walk a little faster until we reach the door of Handyman Haven.

The bells jingle when we open the door, and George and the gossip brigade stand by the cash register—gossiping about something, no doubt. Who knew a bunch of war veterans would be the biggest nosy nellies in town? All five of them look at us with a mix of interest and skepticism.

"Great. Might as well start the rumor ourselves," Jed murmurs.

"Relax. Everyone knows neither of us are settling down material." I lead us over to the paint samples. I widen my arms along the wall of color samples. "Pick your color, Emilia."

"What?" Jed's head whips in my direction.

"She needs a room that she loves. We're going to paint her room."

"We are?"

I nod. "Yep."

"And you decided this, did you?"

"I did." I wait for his reaction, hoping it's not anger. Maybe I overstepped, but I know this is something he's wanted to take care of anyway. And now I can help.

"Why do I have a feeling it's going to be me painting while the two of you watch?"

Emilia giggles and we look at her. She's staring at us talking.

"I can paint. I'm very self-sufficient," I say.

"Fine." Jed sounds like a grumpy old man. Then again, I have a feeling with the way he grew up, he never did much home remodeling. His dad probably paid someone else to do it.

I bend down to eye level with Emilia. "Pick out a color to paint your room."

She walks forward and scans the wall of colors.

Fifteen minutes later, she's still looking, picking up some samples and putting them back. Every time she picks a sample, I read the name out loud and try to get her to do the same. My endeavor hasn't been very successful. She's whispered a few so low I could barely hear her.

"Why don't we just pick pink and purple, girly colors?" Jed asks, his arms crossed, which makes his biceps pop.

I try to push away the memory of the night I explored his sleeve of tattoos with my tongue, but it's forefront in my mind when I respond. "She has to love it. She has to wake up in that room and fall asleep there every night. It has to speak to her, feel like her own space. And even though her life has gone through an upheaval, this is one thing she can control, even if she's too little to understand."

He gives me a look I can't quite get a read on.

Five more minutes pass and it's clear to me he's growing agitated, but he never tries to rush Emilia. In fact, he shows her nothing but patience.

Finally, she picks up a bright orange sample and holds it out to me.

"This is it?" I ask.

Emilia nods with a huge smile, looking very happy.

"Then let's get it." I bend down to her level. "Can you say orange?"

"Arenje," she says.

"I'll take it." I slide my hand into hers, and we go to get her paint mixed.

Twenty minutes later, we have our paint, brushes, rollers, and all the other supplies we need, along with a somewhat annoyed Dad who paid the bill.

Orange was a surprise, but what a girl wants, a girl gets.

Jed's gaze meets mine.

Just not this girl.

Jed

"I guess she won't need a nightlight," I say, rolling the paint on the first wall.

I wanted to switch up Emilia's room, but I'm not really on board with this. What was wrong with the beige walls? Plus, we had to move all the furniture into Cade's old room to make room to paint. We're two hours into this and the first speck of paint is only now hitting the wall.

"It's a very bright color," Molly says, standing behind me and soaking in how vibrant the color is on the walls. We're not talking a pale peach tone. This color is full-on orange. "But Emilia loves it, and if you want her to feel comfortable, you have to give her a space of her own. Let her know this is where she belongs now."

"I thought you were just supposed to get her to talk?" I continue to run the roller through the paint then on the wall.

Molly goes around me with a brush and stands on the ladder to edge the wall. "I am, but she has to trust me. Have fun with me. And you too. The other day, I asked her what you guys have been up to and all she said was whoosh." She glances over her shoulder at me.

I'm trying not to look at her, but her ass is literally right at my eye level. I want to lean forward and bite it just to see her reaction. Plus, she didn't bring painting clothes, so she's wearing my sweatpants and an old college T-shirt.

"I took her up to the glacier and a piece fell down into the lake and made the boat rock at the same time she peed her pants." I look around to make sure Emilia hasn't sneaked into the room. She went to the bathroom.

"Really?" Molly laughs. "What did you do?"

"I tried to get her new clothes, but there wasn't anywhere to grab some, so she ended up coming home wet —but she did get some new stuffed animals out of it."

"Score for her."

I watch Molly work on the wall. She's pretty good at this. "I take it this isn't your first time painting a room?"

She dips her paintbrush in the can. "I was very indecisive when I was growing up. Changed my room a lot. Of course, it was always the mistake paints, but that was kind of fun."

"Mistake paints?" I follow her, rolling after she edges.

She smirks at me. "I forgot Richie never had to worry about money."

"Richie?"

"Yeah. You never worried about money, did you?"

I shrug. "No."

My dad does well, and although he wasn't always great about helping my mom, he took care of us, especially me. I had new cars and my tuition for college was paid for. When we lived in Arizona, we had a cleaning lady, and when Nikki wanted to redo her room, an interior designer was hired for the job. But that changed when we moved here. Which was probably the best thing to happen to us.

"Mistake paints are the ones people return because it's not the color they ordered, or maybe something went wrong with the machine and it didn't mix the color properly. They're, like, seventy-five percent off. So I'd pick one of those." She shrugs.

"Huh, I had no idea."

I hear the toilet flush. Emilia walks in the room and watches us for a moment. She didn't come here with a lot of clothes, so I put her in an outfit that was already a little too small on her. I'll have to take her shopping soon.

I pick up a brush, dip it in paint, and hold it out to her. "Want to help paint?"

Her eyes light up and she rushes over, snatching the brush from my hand. I bend down closer to her and try to put my hand over hers to guide her through it, but she pulls her hand back and paints the wall how she wants.

"Okay then." I take a few steps back.

"There you go, Emilia, that's a brush and we're painting. Are you having fun?" Molly steps down to pour more paint in Emilia's little bucket.

I'm completely enamored by how professional Molly is, but then again, I know firsthand that she's a hard worker.

Emilia nods.

"Can you tell me how you feel?" Molly asks, bending down to her level.

Emilia says, "Yes," in a quiet whisper. "Happy."

"That's awesome." Molly holds up her hand for a high five and Emilia smacks it.

We all continue to paint, and thank goodness for tarps, because Emilia is messy.

We're finally on the last wall and I'm ecstatic that this is almost over. Even Emilia looks tired.

Molly climbs down from the ladder. That's the other thing I can't wait to be over—the torture of having her ass in my face. She's decided to tie my oversized shirt in a knot, so I keep getting glimpses of her stomach. The same stomach my tongue has slid up and down.

A wet feeling hits my neck and Molly laughs. She's with Emilia and directing her hand to put a brush of paint on my neck.

"What are you doing?" I ask.

Molly looks at Emilia, and she shrugs. "Sorry." She covers her mouth with her hand. "Whoops."

They laugh, so I take my roller and run it down Molly's arm. Her mouth falls open and she stares at me for a moment before flinging her brush at me, leaving little splatters all over me. I drop the roller, dip my finger in the orange paint, and put a dot on Emilia's nose. Then I go for Molly, but she runs. Of course, I chase her and get her in the corner.

"Truce!" she yells, while laughing.

"No way!" I run my finger across the back of her neck.

She puts her hand there and stares at the orange paint on her fingers with her mouth dropped open. Seems she forgot who started this.

Emilia comes up to me with a paintbrush, laughing as she runs her brush along my bare calf.

"Hey, you guys are teaming up on me!" I fall to my knees to snatch Emilia up in my arms to stop her, but she ends up on my chest, straddling me and using her paintbrush like she's putting makeup on my face. Very poorly.

It doesn't matter though, because the smile on Emilia's face, especially when Molly is encouraging her, makes me not want to make her stop. To enjoy this moment.

Once I'm fairly sure I look like a Florida orange, I pick Emilia up and get the brush from her, then I paint a heart on her shirt.

She giggles as Molly sits next to me.

"Let's fill up that heart." Molly paints in the outline I drew.

When she's done, Emilia hugs Molly. I watch the

exchange as my heart aches because I want that from my daughter. That love that she's giving Molly. But I'm man enough to admit I haven't done a great job of letting Emilia know how much I already love her.

"Oh, thank you, Emilia." Molly squeezes her, then they whisper again.

Getting prepared, I dip my hands in the paint tray and hold them up as a defensive maneuver as they come at me with their brushes.

"I dare you," I say.

Emilia is hesitant, but Molly comes at me full force. When she slams into me, I put my hands right on her ass. Even Emilia laughs.

"Joke's on you, they're your sweatpants," she murmurs in my ear.

"Joke's on you, I just felt your ass." My dick twitches against her stomach.

She backs up, and the mood in the room sobers. *Way to ruin the moment, asshole.*

"Let's finish this wall," she says to Emilia and grabs their brushes off the tarp, handing Emilia's back to her.

We finish the room. It's blinding by the time we're done.

"How about I order some pizza, I'll get Emilia in a bath, then we can eat?" I ask while we're cleaning out the brushes and rollers in the utility sink in the basement.

"I should probably go," Molly says.

"Let me thank you. She's so happy and it's all because of you."

She's silent and I prepare myself for another night alone on the couch after I get Emilia to sleep. "Sure. But when she goes to bed, I go too."

"Sure, you can come into my bed," I flirt.

She sighs. "Jed."

I hold up my hands. "I'm kidding. Sorry, it's hard. I'm used to our flirting."

She turns and heads up the stairs, torturing me with my handprints on her ass. But I remind myself that I never again want to make her feel the way those other guys did. If something were to happen between the two of us again, it has to mean something.

* * *

I give Emilia a bath, and she plays harder than I've ever seen before. Then I shower to get the paint off, and Molly says she'll be fine until she gets home. Crashing on the couch, Emilia barely has one bite of the pizza before she passes out, so Molly and I move into the kitchen.

I pull two beers out of the fridge and uncap and hand her one. We eat our pizza and drink our beer across from one another at the kitchen table for a while.

"I heard your mom is getting married," I say.

She rolls her eyes and puts down her pizza.

I change course after her reaction. "We don't have to talk about it."

Leaning back in the chair, she brings her beer to her lips. "No, it's fine. It's probably a good thing."

"Yeah?"

She shrugs. "I mean, I won't feel responsible for her anymore, but who knows how long it will last."

"Who's she marrying?"

"Some Troy guy? I guess he was my dad's friend back in the day. I think the three of them were in some kind of love triangle when they were young. Now this Troy guy is back and wants to marry her."

"That sounds… complicated. And my mom married my dad's cousin."

She chuckles then picks at the crust of her pizza. "You hate your dad, right?"

Her question throws me. My first instinct is to leave the table. I'm not an open book when it comes to my dad issues. But I force myself to stay put. Molly is easier to talk to than most. "For the most part."

"I hate my mom. There are a lot of issues between us —mostly the fact she let all those men come before me." She shrugs.

"Is that why…" I stop my question because it's stupid and I don't want her to get upset and leave. Especially after she's helped me so much with Emilia today.

"What?"

"Nothing." I sip my beer and take a bite of my pizza.

"Why I live up to my family's reputation?"

I shake my head. "What you do is your business. It's none of mine."

Silence fills the room, and I could kick myself for saying anything.

"When the rumor started, I was so distraught. I didn't do what that asshole said I did." Her voice is low and I can tell she's unsure if she wants to venture down this path. "He made it all up. But when your mom is known for her affairs, it's hard not to be typecast as being the same. After I denied the rumors for a while and no one believed me, I thought why do people care what I do and what's the point of fighting it? And also, why is it okay for guys and not girls? I felt bad about myself for a long time."

"You shouldn't. You're right. Why is it okay for men and not women?"

"Unfortunately, we both know the answer to that." She takes a pull from her beer.

"Why did you go along with it?" I ask.

She huffs. "I have a sexual appetite. Easier to beat them to it and pretend I didn't care, maybe? Own it rather than deny it. I was stupid."

I nod and continue eating. "I get being compared to your parents. I think people think I'm like my dad. That I like variety and can't keep it in my pants."

Her eyebrows raise. "And are you?"

I pause because I've never said this out loud to anyone. "I'm scared to settle down. I saw the pain my mom went through when she found out about my dad's affair, and you'll be surprised to find out, but I never want to hurt someone like that. It broke her. To think I could be responsible for doing that to someone…" I shake my head. "And worse, what if we had children? I don't know if my dad cares or not, but what he did made each of us look at him differently and not in a good way."

"You're not your dad, Jed," she says softly.

I meet her gaze. "And you're not your mom, Molly."

We both nod and bury our heads in our pizza. I didn't realize how good it would feel to tell someone my biggest fear. I'm glad that someone was Molly.

Chapter Twenty-two

Molly

Two weeks pass in a flash. I've worked with Emilia every day I'm off and she's showing so much progress. She's yet to call Jed Daddy, but I'm working on it. But she's answering with yes and no now and communicating what she wants to eat.

But tonight, I have to suck it up and have dinner with my mom and Troy. We're going to Mandi Greene's SunBay Inn restaurant, so I'm curling my hair and putting on a sundress, something I don't usually wear. I tend to be a jeans and T-shirt gal. And although the inn isn't super fancy, it's Saturday and dinner during tourist season is usually more upscale than during the off-season.

My phone dings with a text message, and I stop applying my mascara with the hopes it's my mom canceling our plans.

Jed: *Emilia and I are going to get ice cream. Want to join?*

I stare at the text. A text that would've lit me up only weeks ago when Jed and I were hiding our sexcapade. But I'm trying to keep some distance between us, not wanting to step over the friendship line. The problem is, every time I'm with Emilia, Jed is there. I've spent a lot of time and shared a lot of meals with them. More than is probably appropriate.

Me: *Sorry, going to dinner at the inn with my mom and her new guy.*

The three dots appear immediately.

Jed: *Order a salad.*

Me: *Why?*

Jed: *Doesn't take long to prepare. Lol*

Me: *Thanks for the tip. We're still on for the zoo tomorrow? I think Nikki wants to come.*

Jed: *I heard something about that. Yeah, we'll pick you up at nine a.m. sharp tomorrow.*

Me: *K, bye.*

Jed: *Bye*

I continue to get myself ready, and when I'm done, I look in the long mirror in my bedroom, happy with my appearance. Since my mom said she'd meet me at the inn, I grab my keys and leave the house.

When I reach the restaurant, I spot the same car that was in my driveway two weeks ago. I sit in the driver's seat for a moment, resting my head on the steering wheel.

This is a good thing. She's going to be married and you'll no longer be responsible for helping her pay the mortgage.

That's true, but it creates a new problem for me—I need to find another place to live. I'm sure they're either going to move into our house or sell it to move wherever he lives.

I inhale again and open the door, shoving my keys in my purse.

Mandi's at the hostess stand when I walk in. Her red hair is twisted in a braid to the side and she's wearing a nice sundress and sandals. "Hey, Mol."

"Is my mom here already?" I ask.

"She is. I put you guys outside. More distractions with the bay." She smiles.

"Thanks."

"I'm here if you need me. Just don't break any dishes." She chuckles and hugs me.

I anchor myself to Mandi, my feet not wanting to move. Then I see a familiar little girl coloring at a table behind her.

"Emilia!" I can't help the excitement in my voice. Seeing her lifts my spirits.

She looks up and is just as excited to see me. She hops off her seat and comes to my side, hugging my legs.

I bend down to her level. "What are you doing here?"

She points at the door leading to the patio. "Outside."

I poke her belly. "Good job using your words. Who is outside?"

Mandi picks up Emilia, securing her to her side. "You'll find out. I'm on aunt duty for a while."

"What?" I shake my head.

Mandi shrugs and pretends to zip her lips. Emilia watches Mandi intently, mimicking her aunt, even throwing away the key.

"What am I going to do with you two?"

I walk across the restaurant and out the door, stopping when I see who's seated across from my mom and a man who's bald but appears in good shape for his age.

Jed.

"What are you doing here?" I ask.

Jed stands and pulls out the chair for me. "I'm in desperate need of adult conversation and your mom said it was okay if I join you guys."

I move to sit, and he tucks me in. I'm so shocked to see Jed, I miss my mom's introductions to Troy.

"I'm sorry." I extend my hand to shake his. The callouses don't surprise me. Not a lot of men around Sunrise Bay don't have them.

"It's nice to meet you, Molly." Troy smiles in a non-creepy way, which is a relief. There've been plenty of times over the years when my mom's flavor of the week looked at me with interest.

"You too."

"I was just telling them all the great things you're doing for Emilia," Jed says.

The waiter comes over, giving me a moment to compose myself. I pretend to drop my napkin while my mom and Troy discuss the specials.

Jed follows me down to pick it up. I'm not sure where this chivalrous creature came from.

"You don't have to do this," I whisper.

"I know. I want to." He swipes up my napkin and hands it to me.

We order dinner and Jed fills a lot of the awkward silence by talking about what we've been doing over the last few weeks. Troy finds humor in almost everything Jed says—or he's faking it to be nice. But Jed is a pretty funny guy.

The bay is beautiful this time of year. A few people are still sprinkled along the beach, soaking up the sunlight. A slight breeze coasts across my bare shoulders and I wish I'd brought a light sweater.

I sip my wine, and my mom clears her throat. *Here we go…* My fingers squeeze the wineglass stem so hard, I fear it might shatter.

"I wanted to let you know that Troy and I are going to elope," she says.

"Destination wedding?" Jed asks.

My mom smiles. "Actually, the courthouse. I'm pregnant."

I spit out my wine, which lands on Troy. He uses his napkin to wipe his face. If he's upset, he doesn't show it.

"You're joking?" I ask.

She shakes her head, and as if this were a movie, she and Troy reach for one another's hands. I glance at her drink. How did I not notice she didn't order alcohol?

"I just found out," Mom says.

"I can't believe you're not in menopause." I balk.

My mom had me when she was very young, so yeah, I guess it's possible she can still get pregnant, just not probable. It's not anything I ever would've expected, other than the fact that my mother isn't responsible and it seems that has once again led her down a path she probably wouldn't choose for herself.

"A lot of women are having children later in life." My mom shoots me her mom look. The one that says, "Stop being like this and smack on a smile."

"Not when the AARP card is about to arrive in the mail," I mutter.

"Molly, stop," she snipes.

I glance around. Jed reaches under the table and puts his hand on my knee, spurring me to look at him. He smiles and signs for me to breathe.

"I'm sorry. I'm just surprised." I take another sip of my wine.

"Of course you are," Troy says in an attempt to smooth things over. "I want to let you know, Molly, I couldn't be happier about this. I've always wanted a child of my own."

"Good to hear. So when are you going to the court-house?" I want to move this along. I glance at the door that leads inside the restaurant, wishing the waiter would return with our dishes.

"In a month. Troy has to go back out on the boat and we have to get the house ready."

I close my eyes, hearing the words I knew were bound to come. We live in a small two-bedroom house. I'm not naive enough to think they want my mom's thirty-year-old daughter living there.

"So is this dinner, like, my notice?" I ask with too much snark in my tone, but I'm not sure why she had to pretend this was a dinner for me to get to know Troy when she's making announcement after announcement.

She looks surprised. "You can stay as long as you want. The baby will be in a bassinet at first anyway, and Troy is on the boat a lot."

"Yes, I'm at sea more than I'm on land. At least it seems like that most of the year." He squeezes my mom's hand.

I smile, but I'm sure it doesn't come close to reaching my eyes. "It's fine. I graduate next month, then I'll find a place."

"No need to be a martyr, Molly. I'm giving you time, but you *are* thirty. I mean, Jed, you're not living with Marla and Hank still, right?" She laughs. The sound of it is like nails on a chalkboard to me right now.

"Yeah, but I live in Hank's old house, so… Molly can come live with us," Jed says.

I scoff. "I'll be fine."

Hell, my best friend lives in a huge house on the bay. Surely she'll put me up for a little bit if necessary.

"I have plenty of room," Jed says. "It's just Fisher, Emilia, and me. If you feel more comfortable, there's the room above the garage. Presley stayed there for a while."

Yes, I remember, and now she's going to marry Cade. I cannot live with Jed. I might as well poke my eyes with chopsticks every day the rest of my life.

I pick up my wineglass. "I'll be fine. I can manage."

"That's probably a good idea," Troy says to Jed.

"I'm not sure. I mean, it's Jed," my mom says to Troy.

"Mom!" God, she is the worst.

"Well, he has a reputation," she says. "And you've always had that crush."

My face heats. She cannot be doing this to me right now.

Troy gives Jed a macho look as though he's congratulating him. Gross.

The anger that was simmering below the surface boils over. "May I remind you that you have a reputation too, Mom?" I lower my voice, but I'm sure they all heard me.

"It's fine. I know I have one, but I'm a dad now," Jed says in an effort to smooth things over.

I shake my head. "Sometimes having a kid doesn't matter, right, Mom?"

"Molly, I know this is all a shock, but there's no reason to speak like that to your mother." Troy squeezes my mom's hand and looks me square in the eye.

I put up my hand. "Troy, you've been here about a hot minute, okay?"

"Maybe we should go for a walk." Jed pushes his chair back from the table.

"Sit down," I seethe through my teeth. I lean in close to my mom, looking at both ends of the table to make sure no one is standing there before I dig into her. "You know nothing about Jed, so you have no right to speak about him like that. Especially since he did me a huge solid by being at this dinner so I didn't have to endure it by myself. And if you want to throw stones, I have boulders of bad shit I can start rolling down the hill. What do you think it was like going to school and having someone come up to me to accuse you of ruining their family because you slept with their father? Or having a classmate joke that they'd slept with you and me never really being sure whether it was true or not?" I snatch my napkin from my lap and toss it on the table before I stand. "Keep his name out of your mouth." I finish off my wine with a dramatic flair and slam the glass down. "Congratulations, you two. Try to do better with this one, Mom."

Without waiting for her to reply, I stomp off the patio and into the restaurant, then I head down the stairs to the bathroom, my hands shaking and my heart racing.

"Holy shit!" Jed comes up behind me. I turn around to face him, but he swoops me up in his arms and swings me around. "That was awesome. Thanks for coming to my defense."

I shake my head, wrapping my arms around his neck. God, he feels good. "She has no idea what she's talking about."

He lowers me to the floor. "I meant what I said. You have a place with us."

"Thank you, but I'm hoping I don't have to take you up on that offer."

"I kind of hope you have to." He grins.

"Jed…"

"Hey, you two, someone saw you and isn't letting me distract her anymore." Mandi walks into the hallway with

Emilia in her arms, Emilia's arms outstretched in our direction.

Jed takes her from his sister. "How about some ice cream now?"

Emilia says, "Yay!"

"Will you join us?" he turns to ask me.

I'm a total sucker. Even if my heart breaks. "I'd love to."

We leave the inn looking like the family we aren't, but I have no regrets. What I told my mom was a long time coming and I breathe a little easier now.

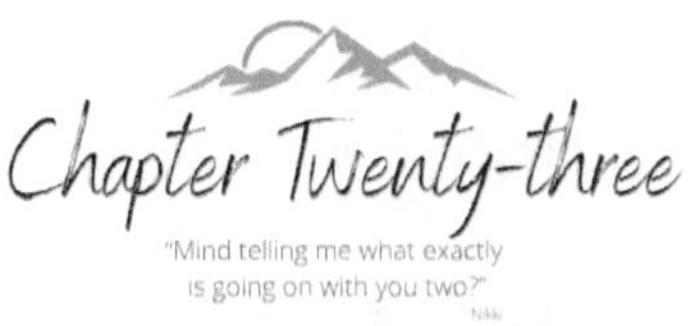

Jed

Emilia and I pull up at Molly's house to pick her up for our visit to the zoo, and Molly's out the front door before I put the truck in park. Instead of climbing in next to me, she opts for the back seat with Emilia.

"Are we still playing this game?" I ask when she files in and says good morning to Emilia.

"Hi," Emilia says in the sweetest voice ever.

I've grown to love hearing her talk.

"I'm still here for Emilia," Molly says, buckling in.

I blow out a breath. "Fine." I put the truck in reverse and pull out of the driveway.

Driving to the zoo, Emilia falls asleep because she didn't sleep great last night, and Molly distracts herself on the phone.

"How are things at your house?" I ask. After the horrible dinner last night, I imagine they're awkward at best.

I told her I went to that dinner to try to pay her back for all the help she's giving me with Emilia, but a part of me just wanted to be there with her. To help her through something I knew she would struggle with.

Molly shrugs. "She's ignoring me. We'll see when she

actually talks to me again. Can you believe she's pregnant?"

I can't, but I don't want to add gasoline to the fire already burning between them. "It's surprising," I answer as honestly as I can.

"Why would they not use protection? It's a classic move for my mom, giving a guy anything he wants. Can she ever put herself first?" She stares out the window and shakes her head, the anger pouring from her once more. "I hate that I'm like her."

"You're not like her," I say, looking at her through the rearview mirror.

"You don't have to sugar talk me. I know I am."

I pull onto the side of the road and put the truck in park before turning to look directly at her. "You are not. When you thought I was using you, you stopped it between us. Nothing has deterred you from getting your degree. And even with all my flirting, you still put the brakes on because you're putting yourself first, so don't put yourself in her category. Got it?"

The most beautiful smile transforms her face, and my heart pricks from the happiness that my words put it there. "Is that a compliment?"

I tilt my head and she laughs. I put the truck in drive and pull back onto the road.

A few miles down the road, she says, "Thanks, Jed."

Our eyes catch in the rearview mirror. "You're welcome."

We arrive at the zoo and Nikki and Logan are waiting for us. Seems they've dragged Rylan along too, but he doesn't look enthused to be here.

Taking out the stroller, I realize I haven't had to use this yet. "We'll be fine without it, right?" I ask Molly.

She shrugs. "She might get tired."

"I can carry her," I say.

"Through the entire zoo?" Her skepticism and doubt are blatant in her facial expression.

"Fine." I hand Emilia to Molly, and of course, Emilia happily goes. Bending over the stroller, I try to figure out how to get it open.

"There must be a latch or something," she says.

I look at her. "Thank you. I know that much."

Molly shrugs and continues playing with Emilia, poking her belly and making her laugh.

"Damn it." I say, removing my finger after it gets pinched between two metal pieces. I abandon the stroller on the ground.

"Daddy is dramatic," Molly says.

I stare at her with both hands on my hips, my finger throbbing.

"Here." Molly hands me Emilia and picks up the stroller.

I lean back on the truck and cross my ankles, waiting for her to prove me wrong, but she's struggling as hard as I was.

She presses something but nothing happens. "I thought it was this thing."

"What's going on?" Nikki comes over.

"How many of you does it take to open a stroller?" Rylan rolls his eyes, scouring the area for anyone watching. The strife of a thirteen-year-old. I wish I had his problems.

"It's a contraption. At this point, I don't even know if I trust it enough to put Emilia in it," I say.

Nikki takes the stroller from Molly, and a second later, it's open. "Seriously, you two." She shakes her head.

"Impressive, babe." Logan kisses his wife on the temple.

"I just picked out our stroller and practiced with each one to make sure I could do it." She shrugs as if it's no big deal, but seriously, I'm impressed. "Now can we please go? I have to pee."

We quickly move Emilia into the stroller and buckle her in, and Rylan reluctantly agrees to push her.

We're not even at the first exhibit before Nikki brings up a date she wants to set Molly up on, which gets my attention. Rylan is talking to me about his soccer tournament and how they're bringing Calista onto their team because another teammate broke his ankle. I'm only half listening because I want to hear Molly's reaction to being set up by my sister. We've grown closer over the last few weeks, and I swear I feel a shift between us. That's not to say I'm going to ask her out—I promised I wouldn't pursue anything with her unless I was serious about it—but I don't want her with anyone else either.

"He's really nice and he works out at the gym with Logan. He's new to town and I told him about my friend who could show him around." Nikki's smile is wide as she waits on her best friend's answer.

Molly catches me listening, and I divert my gaze, concentrating on Rylan.

"Calista's a great player. You guys should be in good shape then, no?" I say.

Rylan talks about his coach and Calista being favored and how the boys don't want to play with a girl. It's like nothing has changed since I went to school.

"I'm not sure, Nik, my plate is full with graduation and stuff," Molly says.

Attagirl. I bite my lip to stop from smiling. Poor Logan is the only one entertaining Emilia, who we took out of the stroller when we arrived at the tiger exhibit. He has her right by the fence and keeps roaring over and over. He needs the practice anyway.

"Don't let her fall in!" Nikki shouts.

Logan turns around with narrowed eyes. He pretends to lose his grip on Emilia but catches her.

"Hey, you can play that game with your own kid, not mine," I scold him.

He laughs and turns around, roaring again.

"Logan, say tiger," Molly yells.

I look at her and our eyes meet. We exchange a smile and my stomach fills with a weird, unfamiliar sensation. It reminds me of coasting down the track of a roller coaster. What the hell is that?

"I mean, Calista is good," Rylan says.

I side-eye Rylan.

"Okay, she's really good," he relents.

I'm not sure what's happening with Rylan and Calista. She was at the summer bash and they were getting along, but he's adamant that he doesn't like her. He's thirteen now and I'm sure the hormones are kicking in, so I'm not sure I believe him.

"Come on, Mol, I already promised him." Nikki's voice pulls me back to their conversation.

"Who is he again?" Molly asks, and I'm happy to hear the annoyance in her tone.

"Ugh, will you listen?" Nikki groans as we all follow Logan to the next exhibit.

Rylan hands the stroller to Nikki. "I look ridiculous pushing an empty stroller."

We all shake our heads, but we remember the days when the smallest thing would embarrass us.

Logan sets Emilia down and she runs toward the next

exhibit—the elephants. Chasing her, Logan swoops her up and she giggles.

One other thing that's happened in the last couple weeks is that Emilia seems to be coming into her own. The bad dreams happen less often, and she's much more communicative. She's making a lot of progress.

She and Logan try to mimic elephant noises as the four of us bring up the rear.

"Say elephant, Log," Molly says. "Point out the water, the trees. And if she points, you tell her what it is and see if she'll repeat it."

"Look at you, Miss Speech Therapist." Nikki knocks her elbow into Molly.

"She's incredible," I say before I can stop myself.

"Stop it. I'm doing what I agreed to," Molly responds.

Nikki's footsteps slow down. I know she's watching us, so I purposely move a foot away from Molly, so as not to activate Nikki's crazy gossip sensors.

"No fucking way," Rylan says, stopping in his tracks.

Nikki smacks the back of his head. "Ry!"

He holds his head, still staring forward. "Sorry."

I follow his vision and a rough laugh flies out of me. Standing right in front of us is Calista with her family.

"Stop it, Jed," Rylan mumbles.

"Come on, it's funny," I say. "I mean, what are the odds?"

"Go say hello." Nikki nudges him like the mom she's training to be.

He shakes his head. "No."

Calista waves, and Rylan lifts his hand in a half wave.

"Go," Nikki pushes. When Rylan doesn't move fast enough, she pinches the back of his arm.

Oh, I see what kind of mom she's gonna be.

Nikki takes Rylan to talk to Calista Bailey and her

family while I stay back with Molly. Logan's now pretending to be an elephant with one arm out, going up and down like the trunk.

"He's going to be a great dad," I say, watching Emilia mimicking him.

"Yeah." Molly leans against the black iron fencing with me.

"So are you going to let Nikki set you up?" I ask, unable to stop myself. It's none of my business, but I want to know.

She shrugs. "I don't know. She already promised."

"So that's a yes?" *Cool it,* I scold myself.

"Is there a reason I shouldn't?" she asks.

That's the big question I'm still trying to figure out. The one I'm asking myself because I've never felt jealous before, but when Nikki brought up Molly going on a date, I wanted to wrap my arms around Molly and scream, "Mine!" like when we were young and fighting over the last donut.

"I'm not sure." I'm trying to be honest. We should probably talk about what's transpiring here.

"Oh," she says, looking disappointed. Or maybe that's wishful thinking on my part.

"I mean—"

Emilia's cries pull me from our conversation, and my gaze tears to where she was with Logan. But she's not there anymore. They're not there. I scour the area quickly, finding Emilia running toward me.

"Dada!" she yells, tears running down her face.

I bend to the ground as she runs right into my arms. I pick her up, soothing her with my hushed shhs and a hand running along her back.

"It's okay." I'm acting as if I have it all together, but I'm reeling from the fact she called me Dada. My mind is racing while a warm sensation fills my chest and I hug my daughter tightly.

Molly comes over, tears in her eyes and a huge smile on her face. She's staring at me because she knows exactly how much it means to me that Emilia called me Dada, that she ran to me for comfort.

It might be stupid, but I've never felt like this before, never wanted to protect someone as much as I do Emilia. When she was screaming and I couldn't find her for that split second, my stomach dropped.

"Is she okay?" Logan comes over. He's trying to see her, concern in his own features. Like I said, he'll be a good father. "One of the bears growled at another one and she freaked out."

"Did the bear scare you?" I ask and she nods into my neck. I continue to soothe her.

Molly is right at my side, her hand on Emilia's back. "Oh, I see cotton candy."

Emilia turns her head to face Molly, and I move my body to show Emilia the cotton candy stand. She squirms in my arms the minute she sees it and I lower her back to the ground. Molly takes Emilia's hand and they walk over to the cotton candy stand.

"Mind telling me what exactly is going on with you two?" Nikki asks as soon as she returns from saying hello to Calista's family.

I face her and open my mouth but shut it. Her eyes remain wide, waiting for me to answer. I wish I could explain it. But the truth is, I don't even know myself.

Molly

I'm at Truth or Dare, packing up the last of what we'll need, while Jed fills the truck with the beer and seltzer samples. We're heading over to Northern Lights Retirement Home for a taste test night that Ethel and Dori set up. I'm not even sure if elderly people should be drinking that much. Aren't they all on medication?

"Good luck over there," Cade says, laughing as he walks into the office.

"What does that mean?" I follow him. "And I'm not sure why I have to go. Aren't you co-owner and her actual grandson?"

He sits in his chair, leaning back with his fingers locked behind his head. "Hey, I had to do a game night once with Presley. Let's just say there's a reason she requested you and Jed go together." His eyebrows waggle.

After Nikki's twenty questions the other night on what's happening with me and Jed, I'm sensing every Greene has their own opinion about what happens after Emilia goes to sleep. But joke's on them, because I usually just go home. Sure, sometimes we have a late dinner. One time we watched *Bar Rescue* together because we both love it. But I absolutely am not sleeping with Jed.

I put up my hand. "I don't even want to know what that means."

"You know exactly what it means."

Cade tips his head behind me, but he doesn't have to alert me to Jed's appearance. I feel him in every cell of my body, and that's why shivers are pricking the back of my neck.

"Ready?" Jed asks. The closeness of his voice only deepens my awareness.

I circle around and plaster on an easy smile. "Ready."

"See you, Cade," Jed says.

I wave, ignoring the expression Cade's giving me.

Outside, Jed opens the passenger door for me, but I stare at it.

"Emilia isn't here," he says with annoyance.

"Yeah, but that spot signifies something." So I step aside and open the back passenger door.

He groans. "Molly, you're way overthinking this passenger seat thing. And I'm not a chauffeur."

"I just don't..." I sit in the back seat and close the door.

As he rounds the front to the driver's seat, I know I'm being stupid. Before the whole hookup thing, I never would've thought twice about riding up there. But I can't be that close to him right now, especially since my feelings for him are intensifying. It'd only spur me to cross that line with him again and end up hurt or imagining what life would be like as his girlfriend. And we all know Jed Greene doesn't do girlfriends.

He turns the key in the ignition, grumbling the entire time about how stupid this is and it's just a seat.

I interrupt his rant to try to change the subject. "Where's Emilia?"

"Fisher's watching her."

"Fisher?" I ask. He seems good with her, but I'm surprised he's down for watching her on his own.

"I have confidence he can handle it. He is sheriff after all."

"I guess. Is Allie joining him?" I ask.

"Not that I know of."

"What's up with those two?"

He shrugs. "From what I know, they're just friends. There haven't been overnight visits if that's what you're asking." He looks at me through the rearview mirror.

I can't help but think he's remembering the times I spent the night. The man knows his way around a bed and a woman's body. "I wasn't. The sheriff's business is none of mine."

"It's Fisher. Sometimes I can't even believe he's a sheriff." Jed shakes his head.

I know where he's coming from. Fisher wasn't exactly a rule follower back in high school. He might even hold the record for the most detentions.

We laugh and continue talking about Nikki and Logan at the zoo the other day. How they'll be great parents, but how we foresee a lot of bossing around by Nikki. The time passes quickly.

He pulls into Northern Lights Retirement Home and parks under the overhang to unload all the bottles. I meet him around back of the truck. He grabs a cooler and carries it inside while I take the cups and a few snacks we had the kitchen prepare so these senior citizens aren't drinking on empty stomachs.

We're not even done getting everything set up when Ethel comes into the events room to inspect our work.

"You need to put everything together. Why are there two tables?" she asks.

"Molly's going to run one and I'm going to run the

other?" Jed fills her in on our plan, which was mostly his idea. I just want this over with as fast as possible so I can put some distance between us.

"No. No. No." Ethel shakes her head and I'm getting a good glimpse of what kind of mother she was to Hank when he was younger. "You're not the only ones coming in. It's a huge thing. This is your area." She points to the side where we'll literally be on top of one another while serving.

"Bibi…" Jed sighs and his head falls back. "You didn't tell me we were one of many vendors. This space is so small."

His fight is for naught, because Ethel starts moving the tables all by herself. I rush to help her because she shouldn't be doing it at all, let alone by herself.

"Don't worry, you're the only beer people. There are some wineries, and we have some restaurants too."

"Just let me do it," Jed grumbles and sets up the table exactly how she wants him to.

"Can we push the table out?" I ask, since my ass is almost plastered to the wall. I nudge the table a bit, but Ethel nudges back. Damn, she's strong for her age.

"No. We need room for walkers, wheelchairs, and scooters. You don't want someone crashing into your table." She beams at me and I have no choice but to nod. "Now I have to go get ready."

We watch her walk out, then we push the table forward a little bit.

"Man, she's bossy," I say.

Slowly, more people come in and set up their tables. Jed's making connections with a few vendors while I finish setting up, then I keep myself busy on Instagram. I pause on a picture of Emilia and Jed on his feed. They're side by side, puffing out their cheeks with wide eyes. It's sweet, and you can see the similarities between them.

He's come so far with her. I was just as happy as he was when she called him Dada at the zoo. And after she said it once, she kept saying it. Every time she found something exciting or wanted his attention, she didn't just tug on his jeans or hit him, she said, "Dada."

"What are you smiling at?" Jed comes behind the table, straightening our bottles.

I turn my phone and show him the picture. His face lights up.

"She's so awesome," he says.

"Well, Jed Greene, how does it feel to be a father?" I hold my phone to his mouth like a microphone.

He chuckles and shakes his head. "Damn good." He leans back on the wall with me. "I never thought it'd feel like this… I can't even describe the feeling. It's like pride that she's mine, a protectiveness over her safety and emotions. How is it that I can't wait until she wakes up in the morning to see what the next day will bring?" He stares at me, looking dumbfounded.

That's all it takes for the deal to be sealed.

Jed Greene has ruined me for any other man. As stupid as it is, and it is stupid, I've fallen in love with him.

A tapping on the microphone interrupts the moment— which I'm grateful for, otherwise I might've blurted out my feelings. We look over to find Leeann, the program orga- nizer, standing in the middle of the room.

"Hello vendors. I wanted to take a quick second to thank you for joining us." She gives the directions and tells us we cannot give more than one sample to the same person.

When she's done, a slew of cane-holding, wheelchair- riding, walker-pushing elderly people enter the large room.

"Let's get this over with," Jed mumbles.

Yes, because his cologne just floated my way, and with the new revelation I just admitted to myself, it only makes him harder to resist. But resist, I will.

Before long, people are at our table. We explain each of the beers we have with us, then pour them whichever one they choose.

"The only question I have is how many will you let me have?" A man with a white mustache and matching hair looks over his shoulder, presumably for Leeann. He downs the two samples we have poured on the table.

"It's only one per person," I say, a little dumbfounded.

He sets his gaze on Jed, and Jed pours another sample for him.

"Jed!" I scold.

"What?" He shrugs.

The man winks at me and walks to the next table.

"Give him a break, he's like eighty-five. What's one more sample going to do to him?" Jed elbows my side.

I get his point, so I don't say anything else.

Ethel leads a couple to the table. "And this is my grand-son, Jed, and his girl, Molly."

"I'm not his girl. I just work for him," I say.

"That's what I said," Ethel says with her forehead furrowed.

"No, you implied—"

"Whatever." Ethel waves me off. Man, she's cranky tonight. "This is Olive and her husband, Bert. Olive doesn't like beer, so I told her to try the seltzer, and Bert wants a beer."

We each pour a sample for them.

"Nice to meet you," I say. "How long have you been married?"

Bert shrugs. "Too long."

He laughs as if it's a joke, and Olive pins her eyes on him as though she wants to strangle him.

"Fifty-seven years," she says with a sharp nod. "This fool took forever to propose. All my friends were having babies and this guy waited until I almost accepted a proposal from someone else."

"I saw you give Isaac more than one." Bert nudges his cup toward Jed, ignoring his wife.

Jed fills it.

I roll my eyes at Jed, then turn back to the woman. "Well, fifty-seven years is a long time. Congratulations."

Olive sips the seltzer and cringes. "Too bubbly." She sets it down.

"Don't be rude, Olive," Bert says and downs her drink while holding his now empty cup out to Jed, who refills it again.

"Jed," I say, exasperated.

"See!" Bert points an accusatory finger at me. "Always nagging. Listen to me." He leans over the table, eyeing his wife who is now at the table for the bakery beside us. "Don't ever marry. The regular sex is great, but the nagging and complaining all the time." He shakes his head. "Don't do it to yourself."

"Get out of here, Bert!" Dori shouts from behind him, then nudges him to get moving. "Do not tell other people your opinion because you're a grumpy old man."

Bert glances over his shoulder and grunts. "Dori." He looks at Jed again. "The worst part is that the men are outnumbered here. How can some of them still not want to have sex? Lesbians, I tell you."

Dori shakes her head. "Maybe there's no one here worth the STD scare."

"Oh, I know what's going on in that sewing room. Clothes for grandkids. Sure, whatever."

"Bert, go find Olive," Dori snipes.

He shakes his head and follows his wife. She's already three tables down, complaining the whole way. The cake next door was too sweet, and now the nuts are too crunchy —she could break her tooth and she has her original teeth, a small miracle.

"Don't listen to him," Dori says. "My husband and I had a great marriage."

"He makes me think you guys are hard on the men around here," Jed says and laughs.

"Nah, they just all think there should be an orgy every night." Dori takes her sample and continues down the way.

Jed and I both look at one another with wide eyes.

"Who would've thought all the action was at Northern Lights Retirement Home? We've been wasting our time," he says.

I laugh and shake my head at what we just witnessed, but a strand of my hair gets stuck on my lips. Jed brushes his finger along my cheek, removing it. Our eyes lock. The way he's looking at me… I can't be imagining it. It doesn't feel like a guy who just wants to hook up, and that's dangerous. So I panic.

"I have a date on Friday," I blurt.

Chapter Twenty-five

Jed

Molly's at my house, working with Emilia, and I'm downstairs, preparing dinner. Tonight is my usual affair of chicken nuggets and macaroni and cheese.

When they come down to join me, Molly laughs. "One day you're going to have to eat like an adult."

"I do. She doesn't." I point at Emilia, who's already getting up on her booster seat.

"She needs to learn to eat adult meals. Like real chicken or how about a vegetable once in a while?"

I put down the bowl of mac and cheese. "Well, I don't like vegetables either."

She nods as though she already knew that. I get a glass of milk for Emilia, then we both sit at the table.

"You're telling me you know what I like?"

"I do," she says in a cheeky way.

"You do not," I protest.

It's nice how Molly just sits and eats without me having to invite her to do so anymore. When she first started helping Emilia, it was uncomfortable, mostly because of us hooking up prior. Now it feels natural, and Molly is here more than she's not. But that might all change since we're getting to the end of her case study.

"You hate broccoli." She splays her fingers out and pushes down on one using her other hand.

"Everyone hates broccoli." I roll my eyes.

Emilia laughs. She loves it when we're like this, as though she understands our jokes.

"Not everyone, but let me continue."

I wave my hand for Molly to finish while I spoon mac and cheese onto Emilia's plate.

"You eat the quesadillas at the brewery, but you don't want onions or tomatoes."

I shrug. "Everyone has preferences."

She laughs and points her fork my way. "But you would eat like this for the rest of your life if you could."

"Hello, I eat every kind of fish there is. I eat crab, lobster, pretty much all of our local stuff from the water."

"I'll give you that. But you're only getting older, Jed, and you only have one heart."

She starts eating while I cut up Emilia's chicken nuggets that will likely end up more in her lap than in her mouth.

"Dada!" Emilia exclaims, holding out a spoonful of her mac and cheese.

She likes to feed me and I'm starting to figure out it's so she doesn't have to eat. She wants to be out of her booster seat and playing all the time. But because I please her any way I can, I lean forward and let her shovel a spoonful into my mouth.

"Like father like daughter." Molly smiles brightly at us.

I groan, putting the chicken nuggets on Emilia's plate before starting in on my own. "All right, how about you make us dinner and I promise to eat all of it."

Molly doesn't even take a moment before agreeing. "Deal."

I probably like the fact that we're making plans for the future a little too much.

Emilia eats a bit and wants out before we're finished, so I clean her up and she heads to the family room to play with the new ball pit I bought her.

"Are you all ready for your date?" I should keep my mouth shut, but I haven't been able to stop thinking about it since she told me two days ago. I told her it was good when she said it, the exact moment I would've kissed her if we weren't in the Northern Lights Retirement Home.

She sighs. "Nikki already promised the guy, so I feel like I don't have a choice. But the truth is, I don't want to go." Using her fork, she moves the macaroni around on her plate.

"I'm sure it'll be fun. She'd never fix you up with a douchebag." Each word cuts me, but Molly made it clear that we weren't compatible. Although I feel as though that's changed, I'm not sure how she feels.

"I guess we'll find out." She slides her chair out and picks up her plate. "I should probably get going. I'll wash the dishes first though."

I follow her to the sink, peeking into the family room to make sure Emilia is good. She's watching a show and sitting in the ball pit. Sometimes it's scary how fixated on the TV screen she can become. It's like the world around her doesn't exist.

"I'll clean up dinner."

"How about we do that together?" she offers.

I'm not going to turn down spending more time with her, so I agree. We talk about Emilia and her case study during the dishes. How Molly's professor wants to meet Emilia because from the short videos Molly's filmed, he's impressed how fast Emilia's progressing. What can I say? She's a Greene after all.

"I think a lot of it was just her becoming comfortable, to be honest," Molly says, placing a dish in the dishwasher after I rinse it.

"Little kids have such resilience. I still have a lot of decisions to make as we move forward. One of which is when to talk to her about Tanya and share memories of her with Emilia. I mean, I'm fairly sure she won't remember—"

"No, I don't think she will," Molly says. "I mean, what's your first memory?"

I shrug. I'm not sure I've ever thought about it, but probably nothing before age five. I think any memories from before that just come from stories that were shared. Like when I pushed Nikki's bassinet down a hill because I didn't like her. Obviously she's fine now, but she loves to tell people that story. How my mom went running and caught it before Nikki went into the traffic. I'm sure it must be an exaggeration because I don't remember it.

"Now that my anger toward Tanya has lessened, I only feel bad that Emilia won't have her mom in her life. The day I took her to the glacier, the woman at the store kept telling her the big puffin is the mama. She handed the puffin back to the lady and kept the little puffin and the moose."

Molly clasps her hand over her heart. "You're the moose?"

"I think so, but she never has the moose hug the little puffin." I shrug. Molly frowns, and I chuckle. "It's okay now that she hugs me in real life. But I bought the big puffin anyway because I want her to remember Tanya. I want her to know the feeling of having a mom, you know?" I finish the last dish and hand it to Molly.

"Without marrying someone?" she asks with raised eyebrows.

"Don't put words in my mouth."

She looks up from putting the final plate in the dishwasher.

I step closer, ready to ask her the question that's been on my mind for weeks. "Mol—"

"Dada!" Emilia runs into the room, her feet sliding on the floor. She falls to her butt and slides a few feet across the floor.

"You good?" I ask.

She looks dazed and confused when she stands, but she recovers quickly. "Wee!" She slides on the floor in her socks.

"I see a whole new phase coming in," I say to Molly with a smile.

Molly joins Emilia, and I dry my hands, admiring the two most important girls in my life. I owe Molly so much because I definitely wouldn't be the dad I'm becoming without her straight talk. She gave my daughter the best gift—the ability to communicate and love me.

"Come on!" Molly grabs my hand, circling me around with them.

The sound of a truck engine makes its way closer to the house before turning off. I'm sure it's Fisher, so we don't stop what we're doing. When he opens the back door, he freezes, standing there in his uniform, eyes fixed on us.

"What a cozy little family." He shuts the door, touches Emilia's nose with his finger, and heads upstairs. Ever since Emilia came to live here, he's been extra cautious to make sure the gun is put in the safe right away.

Eventually, Emilia grows tired and lies on the couch in the family room.

"I think it's someone's bedtime," I say. Emilia doesn't even fight me when I pick her up.

"Yeah, she's pretty sleepy. I'll let you get her to bed." Molly turns and starts walking away, but I take her hand.

"Stay. I have something I want to talk to you about."

It's about time I lay out my feelings and we figure out what this is between us, especially before she goes on that damned date on Friday.

"Okay." Her voice is soft. Maybe I'm imagining it, but I swear I see hope in her eyes.

I hurry up and get Emilia changed and ready for bed. She insists on a good night story, so I read her the book she picked out at Presley's store that day. After we're done, she has a habit of taking all her stuffed animals and putting them around her before she lies down to go to sleep.

"Mama," she says. It throws me for a second until she points at the big puffin that's on her dresser. The one she rarely touches. Maybe she overheard me talking to Molly.

I stand, retrieve the puffin, and hand it to her. Emilia takes the big puffin, the moose, and little puffin and puts them into one big pile. The ostrich is still there but not in the circle with the rest. She smiles at me once she has them just right.

"You got everyone you want?"

She picks up the little puffin. "Me." She sets it down and picks up the moose. "You."

I smile, my insides warming.

Then she grabs the ostrich. "Mama."

I'm a little thrown now. I didn't know the ostrich was a person, or represented a person, I guess.

"Who's this?" I pick up the big puffin.

"Mama," she says.

I tilt my head. "If this is Mama." I pick up the ostrich. "And this is mama," I pick up the big puffin. "Two mamas?"

She nods and smiles. I scratch my head, unsure how to ask her what she means, although I have my suspicions.

"You have two mamas?"

She nods again with a big smile.

"You mean a mama and a grandma?" I ask.

"No," she says, her eyebrows furrowed. Picking up the big puffin, she holds it up with the sweetest, most innocent smile. "Molly. Mama."

My heart sinks.

I really screwed this one up.

Molly

The idiot that I am, I decide to eavesdrop on Jed putting Emilia to bed. It's not the first time. It's just so damn cute the way he does all the different voices of the characters in whatever book they're reading. Seeing him becoming the father I knew he could be makes me so happy and proud.

Turning off the lights after he finishes the book, Jed turns on a star gazer I know she loves.

My stomach fills with flutters because he's tucking her in and they're talking about her stuffed animals. Soon he'll be downstairs to talk to me. He seems upset about me going on a date, but then again, maybe he wants to talk about the case study—or worse, maybe he's going to ask me for another one-night fling.

I peek around the corner and see Emilia getting her animals just right, even incorporating the big puffin, which I know is what Jed wanted. My heart broke a little when he said he worried about her forgetting Tanya and how he wants her to remember her mother.

They go over the stuffed animals' names. I inch forward to hear better, addicted to hearing her call him Dada in her sweet voice.

The bathroom door opens down the hall, and a shirtless, towel-wearing Fisher stands there with a heap of steam behind him. We look at one another and he steps over to look into Emilia's room, then back at me with arched eyebrows.

I wave him off. "Oh, go mind your business."

"Um… couldn't I say the same to you?" he whispers.

I shove him and my hand slides off his wet arm. Shaking it, I wipe it down my pants. He laughs and heads to his room.

All I hear is, "Molly. Mama."

My eyes bulge and my throat constricts.

"Aw… baby," Jed says, but nothing else for a beat. "The big puffin is Molly?"

I look around the corner again and see his shoulders sink. Then his head falls forward for a moment.

"Honey, Molly is Molly. I'm not sure she can be your mommy." He looks out her window and murmurs something I can't hear.

Emilia frowns. "Why?"

I want to praise her. I've been teaching her to ask questions if she doesn't understand something. And also, I kind of want to know too, because his words only confirm for me that he didn't want to talk to me later about us, or try to convince me not to go on the date or something.

"It's complicated and you wouldn't understand right now. But you can love Molly… she just can't be your mama."

Emilia's little face scrunches. I know the tears are coming before I see them.

I tiptoe down the stairs, having heard enough and not wanting to hear the bullshit story he'll tell her. Then I grab my bag and walk out of the house.

As I put my hand on the handle of my car door, Jed

opens the front door of the house. "Where are you going?" He steps outside and jogs down the steps.

"I just got my period." I lie with a reason I know he can't help me with. It's a man's house after all.

"Oh, we might have something." His cringe says probably not, so I keep to my story.

"It's fine. I'm starting to get cramps and…" I become distracted as he nears, and I worry I won't be able to lie if he gets too close.

"Why don't you come back? Or…" He glances back at the house. "Fisher's home. I can take you to the store."

Where is the Jed I'm used to? The one who just told his daughter I wasn't mama material? Can he please show up right now?

"It's fine. We can meet up later. How about Saturday before my shift? You can bring her to Truth or Dare and I'll work with her? I've been wanting to take her to Presley's for story time anyway."

He nods but looks me over with a furrowed brow. "Right, because you have that date on Friday." He stuffs his hands into his jeans and rocks back on his heels.

"Yeah."

As he backs away, I feel the wall he's erecting between us, which suits me fine. "See you Saturday. Have fun on Friday night." He waves and stands on the front porch.

I climb into my car and turn the ignition, trying not to look at him. But I allow myself one fleeting glance before backing up and vow not to ever get close to Jed Greene again.

Ten minutes later, I pull up to the big house on the bay and sigh, but she's the only one who will make me feel better. I bite the bullet and get out of my car, then ring the doorbell. I hear her talking behind the door, and she smiles when she opens the door. Nikki always smiles.

"I'm so sorry." Tears spill down my face as I step into her house uninvited, throwing my arms around her.

"Whoa," Nikki says, but takes the weight of me as she always does. "Come in."

I peel myself off of her and she shuts the door, putting her arm around my shoulders and leading me into their family room.

"Log," she says and he looks up from the television.

"Hey, Molly." He takes me in and stands. "I'll give you two some space." He runs his hand down my arm before leaving the room.

"Here. Sit down." She guides me to the sofa and I sit down, unable to look at her, so I keep my vision fixed on the floor. The cushions dip with her weight when she sits next to me. "What do you have to be sorry for?"

"I can't tell you, but I had nowhere else to go." My voice is hoarse already, and I haven't even said much.

She runs her hand down my leg. "Come on, Mol. I'm your best friend, you can tell me anything."

"You're going to think I'm so stupid." I shake my head and cover my face with my hands.

She groans, sighs, then groans again. "Please tell me it's not what I think it is."

I look over and see anger in her features. "What?"

"I knew it. I saw it."

"Saw what?" I ask, wanting her to say it instead of having to confess myself.

"I told you he was an asshole. You've stayed away from him for this long and now..." She shakes her head, then her expression morphs from anger to concern. "He hurt you?"

"It's complicated," I say.

She places her hands on her belly. "Good thing I have all the time in the world." A smile tips her lips.

It's enough to let me get it all out, tell her everything from start to finish. Twenty minutes and a box of tissues later, she knows it all. From the hookups before Emilia's arrival to me calling it off, to all the time we've been spending together lately.

"So now it's gone from lust to love?" she asks, her hands rubbing her belly.

"Yeah, but you know he doesn't want that."

Her eyes shoot up in a "Well, he's an idiot" expression.

"Why aren't you mad?" I ask.

Laughing, she takes a black olive from the tray in front of her. I scrunch my eyebrows as she pops it in her mouth. "Don't judge, cravings. Pickles, olives, and everything else that's canned, I swear."

I chuckle. "I'm really sorry."

She waves me off. "Stop apologizing. You didn't do anything to me. If I'm honest, I kind of thought this would happen."

"What?"

She nods. "You two were always circling one another, even before I came into your life. I was trying to save you from heartache, but it found you anyway."

I sniffle and blow my nose again.

"Sometimes I wonder if I hadn't made it such a big deal for the two of you not to be together, would you guys have even been attracted to each other?"

"What are you talking about?" I scrunch the tissue in my hand.

She sighs and tilts her head. "The two of you always want what you can't have. You're both hell-bent on telling the world that rules are made to be broken."

I shrug in acquiescence and grab a sweet pickle from the tray. "Are you suggesting I wanted Jed just because you stamped him off-limits?"

She nods. "Yeah, but I guess I always knew that wasn't all of it. At least, I did after Jed beat up Matty."

I sit back on the couch and cross my legs. "What? Matty?"

She nudges my leg. "Remember the asshole Matty from high school?"

"Like I'd forget."

"Jed beat him up. He made some comment about how you probably blew Jed behind the concession stand or something and Jed beat him up in the locker room. Almost got suspended. But you know my dad was good friends with Coach and had been buying him off, so the suspension never happened."

I'd heard rumors at the time that something went down between Jed and Matty, but I never knew what it was about. "I had no idea."

"I didn't either until my dad called my mom the night after we first met. Said Jed couldn't be doing stuff like that and expect to get a scholarship to a Division 1 school. I think a piece of me knew then that you two might really have a thing for each other. But then Jed showed his true colors and kept moving from girl to girl, never wanting to settle down, and I figured it was best for you to be apart because I never wanted it to come to a point where you wouldn't want to be friends with me since he's my brother."

I lean my head back on their couch cushion. "Oh, Nik, you're stuck with me no matter what."

She squeezes my hand.

"I can't believe I let myself fall in love with a man who doesn't want a relationship. How stupid am I?"

She grabs three olives, putting one on each finger as if she's five years old. "You think you can control who you love?"

"I could've stayed away from him."

"Mol, you've been working for him for years."

"I've been working for Cade too."

"Let's be honest, you've always wanted to jump Jed's bones." Her body shakes in a wake of shivers. "As gross as that is to think about."

"I can't deny that I've been attracted to him over the years."

"Honestly, it's a surprise you guys have been apart for this long." She eats the olives off her fingers.

"We're not together," I say, reaching for another sweet pickle.

"Not yet, but—"

"He said I wasn't mother material." I throw my head back on the cushion again. "He hit me right where my deepest wound is—that I'm going to be like my mother. Always looking for someone to love me and not cut out to be a parent. Sleeping with men in the hopes they want to stick around, prove to me that I'm loveable. But there were times with Emilia…" I'm embarrassed to admit what I felt.

"That you three felt like a family?"

"I know better than to believe in that shit." I snag another sweet pickle and she grabs some more olives.

"You know, if you weren't my best friend and he wasn't my brother, I would've outed you on Scandals of Sunrise Bay already." She pops the olives into her mouth.

"Shut up."

She nods. "You two were obviously into one another. Being at the zoo with you guys confirmed it. When Jed would watch you with Emilia, I saw it."

"Saw what?" I shake my head because she's talking crazy.

"The way Logan looks at me. Like I'm his world."

I sniff back my emotions when I feel tears build in my

eyes again. "You're insane, Nik. Don't mess with me just to try to make me feel better."

"I take major offense to that. I would not say it just to make you feel better." I don't respond, so she continues, "Listen, I won't lie, the idea of you being involved with my brother scares the crap out of me, but regardless of what happens between you two, you need to know you aren't alone in this. There are feelings on his side too. I'm sure of it."

I look at her while she nods emphatically. But why do I have such a hard time believing that Jed Greene could be in love with me too?

Chapter Twenty-seven

Jed

*M*olly pulls out of the driveway, and I stare after her. I don't understand what the hell just happened. When I walk back into my house, Fisher's on the couch, staring at me.

"What did you do?" He nods toward the driveway where her headlights have now disappeared.

"Nothing." I raise my arms at my sides.

"What's going on with you two?" He stands and heads into the kitchen.

"Nothing."

"Wanna know what I see?" He pulls out leftover pizza and heads back into the family room with it, then drops the pizza box on the coffee table. Obviously, he's going to play video games all night.

"Not really." I go through the mail he must've brought in with him and set on the table because I'm still waiting for the final paperwork concerning Emilia.

"It seems like you guys are playing house."

I flop into the chair adjacent to him and put my feet on the coffee table. I use the same excuse I've given everyone who's asked so far. "She's helping Emilia."

"You know what I always found funny about you?" He

boots up the game system and picks up a piece of pizza while it loads.

"Not really." I'm sure he's gonna tell me anyway.

"You've always thought people are oblivious, like we don't see what you're hiding. So your dad was an asshole who paid people off to give you everything you wanted." He shrugs. "My mom died when I was ten. It sucks, but life is full of twists and turns and you move on."

"I'm not sure I understand what you're telling me here."

Fisher and I aren't really heart-to-heart kind of guys. Usually, he keeps his opinions to himself. He's crazy if he thinks his mother's death hasn't affected him. It's affected each of them, just like my parents' divorce has my siblings.

"You're just scared, and instead of facing that fear, you bury it deep down like people won't see it. But we all see it. Come on, you honestly don't want a wife or a family ever?"

"Isn't this like throwing rocks from your glass house?" I grab a piece of pizza.

"My issue is my job, plain and simple."

"Mine is too," I grumble.

"You run a brewery," he says with a shake of his head. He puts down his controller and shifts to face me. "Listen, I'm telling you this because you're about to fuck it all up. Molly is a perfect fit for you. Hell, you both have buried your issues in other people all these years when you should've had a friends-with-benefits relationship, but denial and all that."

"If I fuck this up, it affects Nikki and everyone else." I blow out a breath.

He nods. "And if you don't fuck it up? Isn't that what you're really scared of?"

I sigh, then smile just thinking about what it could be

like if we somehow made this work. "I'm not stupid, I was gonna talk to her about it tonight. See what she thinks. Get her perspective."

"Her perspective?" He laughs, shaking his head as though I'm an idiot. "You don't need her perspective. You need to convince her you're the only one for her. Win her over. What are you gonna do, build a pro and con list with her?" He picks up the remote.

"I've never had to win a woman over in my life."

Flowers and chocolate seem stupid and not at all like Molly and me.

"Join the club. You think I know how to win her over? I don't. I'm just saying you're supposed to lead with your heart, not your brain." He tosses me a controller and starts the game.

We set up the game while I rack my brain for what I could do.

"Oh, and she overheard you talking to Emilia in her bedroom. That's when she ran out. So whatever you said put you in a pile of shit." He says it so nonchalantly, it takes me a minute to recollect what I was talking to Emilia about.

"Fuck," I murmur.

"How big a pile of shit are you in?"

"A goddamn cow pie."

He laughs and kills me as soon as the game starts.

"You know who you need to talk to first, right?" he asks as I wait for him to finish his game.

I groan. "Nikki."

"Yep."

"Do you have a jock I can borrow?"

He chuckles and glances at me for a moment. "Shit, you might need my Kevlar vest."

"No shit."

We play the game for the rest of the night while I mentally prepare myself to talk to my sister, because she deserves to know what I'm about to do—fight for the woman I love.

The next morning, I drop Emilia off at my mom's because she doesn't need to bear witness to her pregnant aunt kicking my ass. Luckily my mom had planned to work on the campaign from home today. I feel bad that I haven't been able to be more involved in her trying to get elected, but I've had a lot on my plate. Besides, from what I hear, Posey is a pro as her campaign manager.

I ring Nikki's doorbell with the hopes she hasn't headed out yet.

Logan opens the door. "Hey, man. We go from no visitors to the doorbell ringing nonstop."

"Oh yeah? Who else was here?" I step inside.

He shrugs off my question. "Want breakfast or a coffee?"

I follow him into their kitchen, where Nikki is sitting at a table full of platters of food. I stop in the archway, wishing I wasn't here to fight with her so that I could snap a picture and hold it over her head forever.

"I'm eating for two," she mumbles over a mouthful of pancake.

Over by the coffeepot, Logan maneuvers his finger across his throat. I can't imagine what it must be like to live with her while she's pregnant. She's not the easiest going person in the world when she's not growing another life inside her.

"I'll have a coffee." I walk over to Logan, and he pours me a cup.

"I'm out of here because… well, I don't wanna be here." Logan kisses the top of his wife's head and shakes my hand before he goes.

"What does that mean?" I ask Nikki, sliding a chair out from the table and sitting down.

She waves him off. "Don't worry about it. Why are you here?" Her eyes track over the plates and she decides on some eggs. "Have some. I got a little overzealous. Some mornings I can't stand to eat, and others I can't eat enough. I take advantage on days like this."

I watch her pile eggs on her plate. "Not judging. I know nothing about what it's like to carry a baby."

She stops and rubs her belly. "It's a blessing." She smiles, but it doesn't come close to reaching her eyes. "But it's hard to give up your body for nine months, and if I breastfeed, that'll extend it. And then I have to think about the fact that if I do breastfeed, my breasts and my nipples won't ever be the same and what if Logan doesn't like them anymore? And I'm highly sensitive—"

I cover my ears. "Oh my god, please stop."

"Sorry, overshare?" She chuckles.

"Yes. Do you want me to overshare about my sexual escapades?"

"I've heard enough about your sex life, so maybe you're due for a little payback." She forks a pile of eggs and puts them in her mouth.

My forehead wrinkles. "When did you hear anything about that?"

"Try all your girlfriends in high school."

I shake my head. She has no idea what she's talking about.

"Anyway, tell me why you're here," she says.

Delaying, I sip my coffee and our eyes meet across the table. "Who's the guy you're fixing Molly up with?"

She smirks but cuts up some sausage, so I have no idea if she's just excited to eat or what the smirk is for. "Yeah. He works out at Logan's gym. New to town."

"Do I know him?"

Sunrise Bay is small. Usually new people stand out, but then again it's tourist season, so he might not be so obvious.

"No, don't think so." She eats another bite of sausage.

"Well, I want you to cancel her date with him." The words leave me in a rush.

She lowers her fork, wipes her mouth with her napkin, and sets her gaze on mine. "Why would I do that?"

"Because I like her."

She laughs and picks up her fork, shaking her head. "You like her? We've had this conversation, Jed. You're not going to ruin my relationship with my best friend because you like her. You're only going to break her heart."

I push the coffee farther up the table, cross my arms, and lean them on the edge of the table. "I don't really care what you think about this. I'm going to ask her out. I'm going to pursue her." I inhale, waiting for her to go ballistic.

"She has a big heart under that tough exterior."

"I know she does."

"And she's kind, so kindhearted. Plus, you can't just bring someone into Emilia's life and strip them away when you've had your fill—"

"Goddamn it, Nikki, stop!" I yell.

Her mouth hangs open as she stares at me. "I'm just telling you she's not someone you can just play around with whenever the mood strikes."

I stand from the table, unable to remain seated and

calm any longer. "I know my reputation, okay? But every time I'm with her, I don't want her to leave. And when we're apart, I find myself waiting impatiently until she's with me again."

"Hmm. That doesn't sound like 'like' to me." She turns in her chair, abandoning her plate. "Are you sure this isn't just because she's helping you with Emilia? Maybe you're transferring those feelings over to her in a romantic way."

I rest my palms on her breakfast island and stare at Nikki long and hard before I get up the nerve to admit my real feelings for Molly. "I love her, okay? And it scares me shitless. But I do. And sure, I love how she is with Emilia, and Emilia wants her to be her mom, which I'm sure Molly isn't close to ready for. But that's something we can figure out later on. I have to convince her to date me first. To trust me after I've hurt her and convince her that she's loveable."

A smile overtakes Nikki's mouth and her eyes fill. "I've been waiting for you to come to me."

"What are you, the Godfather?" I ask. She's acting like I should kiss her ring.

"I wanted you to fight me for her. To show me you were worthy."

Usually I'd be pissed off, but I like that she's looking out for Molly. Those two are crazy protective of one another, and I'm glad they've had each other's backs over the years.

"I'm not so sure I'm worthy, but I have no choice. If I don't at least try, I know I'll regret it. And the thought of her going on a date with some douche is like a knife in the heart."

"Hey, Log!" she yells.

"Yeah, I'll tell him the date is off," he says, as though he's been listening the entire time.

"Sit down, Jed."

I sit at the table and grab a piece of bacon. "What?"

"You are worthy. You have to stop tormenting yourself because of Dad. He was an asshole, but guess what?"

"What?" I bite off a piece.

"You have a lot more of Mom inside you than you give yourself credit for. You don't hurt people like Dad did. You don't force your agenda or your desires on someone else like he always did. Look at you and Emilia. Once you stepped up, you emerged as a great father. And you can be a great partner in life too. You just have to believe in yourself and stop worrying about turning into Dad because it's not going to happen."

I huff. Easier said than done. "Thanks."

"Now, let's come up with a plan for you to win over my best friend."

I smile. "I have some ideas."

She waves me off. "My ideas will be better."

"Nik…" Log calls from the other room in a scolding tone.

I chuckle.

She rolls her eyes. "Fine, what did you have in mind?"

My heart skips a beat now that everything is coming together, but I still fear that I blew my shot with the only woman I've ever loved.

Chapter Twenty-eight

Molly

I'm getting ready for my date on Friday evening when someone knocks on my bedroom door. I knew my mom was home, but she's been in her bedroom with the door shut, so I haven't had to deal with her.

Mom opens the door a smidge and pokes her head in. "Can I come in?"

"It's your house," I say.

She sighs and walks in, walking over to sit on my bed. I'm on the floor in front of the mirror, putting on my makeup since I didn't want to use the bathroom in case it meant I would run into her. It's childish, but whatever.

"You help me pay the bills, so I guess the house is both of ours."

"Your name is on the—"

"For heaven's sake, Molly, just stop." The anger in her tone throws me a little. "I'm here to apologize, okay?"

I stop putting on my eyeliner and stare into my lap.

"I shouldn't have surprised you like I did at the restaurant. And I probably should've told you about the pregnancy without Troy there. It's just that I'm happy and I want you to be happy too." She rubs her nonexistent belly much like Nikki does her swollen one.

For a moment, I wonder what it will be like if I ever have a pregnant belly, but I doubt I ever will.

"I'm going to be a different mother for this one." Her voice is small.

"Okay." I shrug, trying to push away the pain of being her trial-and-error offspring.

"I'm serious. I know I messed up with you."

"Do you?" I ask and look at her. "Do you have any idea how much you messed me up?"

"I don't expect you to understand my reasons."

I turn around to face her fully. "And what were your reasons? Besides pure selfishness."

Mom sighs and doesn't look at me, her hand continuing to run along her stomach as though it's giving her the strength to get through this conversation. "When your dad left, my world crashed and burned. I didn't know what to do. I was young, and I just wanted to feel like I did when I was with him. I searched out that feeling over and over again, and once I realized I'd never get it again, I decide to shut down, to be numb."

I want to ask why my love wasn't enough, but I don't because the answer doesn't matter. The answer won't change anything.

"Do you know what that did to me? What it was like for me at school?" I try to keep my voice neutral, but the anger seeps in anyway.

"Molly, I understand I was selfish, but I'm apologizing. Will you just accept it?"

I blow out a breath and rise to my feet to grab an outfit for my date. A date I don't want to go on, but Nikki called me earlier to make sure it was a go. She gave my address to the guy even though I told her I would've preferred to meet him somewhere. But she had a point when she said I deserve to be wooed to get Jed off my mind.

"Okay then, apology accepted."

She stands from the bed. "If I could turn back time, I would. But I can't. What do you want me to do?"

"I don't know. Actually feel bad about it? Understand that you ruined my life?"

"You had the Greenes. You didn't need me." Mom goes to my dresser, picks up some of the jewelry there, and looks at it.

"Another family isn't a substitute for my own."

"It sure seemed that way."

"Well, it sure seemed like my love wasn't enough for you."

She turns around with a set of earrings in her hands and her mouth hanging open. "Is that what you think?"

I bury my head in my small closet. "What was I supposed to think?"

"That your mother was a screwup. That she was lost in her own depression and couldn't pull herself together to raise her daughter."

"Well, I didn't. I just figured I was unlovable." My heart cracks with my admission. Isn't that the exact reason I started to live up to my reputation? Because I was chasing the same thing my mom was? In the hopes that someone would say their life was incomplete without me?

Marla was overprotective, sure, but at least Nikki knew her mom loved her and worried about something happening to her. I never had a curfew. No one called if I wasn't home before dark. No one checked my report cards to make sure I had good grades. No one cared enough about me. Ever.

"Oh, Mol." She shakes her head. "You are loveable. Look how the people in this town love you. They don't much care for me, which is understandable, but they love you."

I shake my head. "You have no way of knowing that."

"I love you, Molly. I know I haven't shown it over the years, but you're my daughter."

Tears threaten to spill, and I sit on my bed, abandoning looking for an outfit. "It never seemed like it." I feel the weight of her sitting behind me, and I close my eyes.

"I love you. I've always loved you. I'm completely to blame for abandoning you most of your childhood, and I will harbor that guilt for the rest of my life. But I want us to have a relationship. I want you to be a part of this baby's life." She places her hands on my shoulders.

I swivel to face her. The big question is… can I accept her apology?

"I'm so sorry, honey. I never meant for us to get this way. I wish I could change our past, but I can only promise to do better moving forward." Mom opens her arms and I lean into her, allowing her to hug me. "But you're a great person and anyone would be honored to love you."

I can't remember the last time I hugged my mom, so I sink into it, basking in the feeling of having the woman who gave birth to me be there for me for what amounts to the first time in my life.

"Troy does seem nice," I admit.

She chuckles. "He treats me good. If it wasn't for you, I'd wish I made a different decision back in high school." I draw back, and she tucks my dark hair behind my ear. "But the one great thing I got from your dad was you, and that makes all the shit worth it."

"Really?"

"Yes!" She hugs me again and I inhale deeply.

We stay entwined for minutes, and I make a promise to myself to try to move forward from this point, not drag our past into the present.

"I know it's none of my business, but are you sure about Jed Greene?"

I inch back. "Mom… I think we both know about reputations."

She nods. "I'm hoping I can reverse mine after all these years."

I look at her belly. "You can. This town will let you start over."

"At least I know he or she will have a big sister with her head on straight."

"I wouldn't go that far."

We both laugh.

"So, we're good?" she asks, standing. "I should let you get ready."

"Yeah, we're good."

She places the earrings in my palm. "Wear these. Your father gave those to me and it's time that I part with them."

I look at earrings that resulted in a screaming match between my mom and I when I was in high school. "Maybe we should just burn them."

"Nah, the man is a jackass, but without him, there's no us."

I realize she's right. "True enough, and they are beautiful."

She moves my hair back while I put them on. "That they are."

The doorbell rings downstairs.

"Shoot, I'm not ready. Can you get it?" I ask.

"Take your time. I'll tell him you'll be down in a few."

She leaves the room, and I shut the door to change. Nikki wasn't really clear on where he's going to take me, but she said casual, so I put on my black frayed jeans and a short T-shirt with a light jacket over top. Double-checking myself in the mirror, I pucker my lips, put some more lipstick on, grab my purse, and head downstairs.

I hear my mom talking the guy's ear off while I make my way down. He's probably ready to get out of here. Who lives with their mom at thirty?

"Thanks, Mom, I'm read—" I stare at Jed standing there in a pair of dark jeans and T-shirt and a casual jacket. Not one hair out of place and I smell his cologne from here. "Is Emilia okay?"

"I'm here for you." His cheeks flush.

"I'm going to leave you guys to it. Have fun." Mom smiles as she passes me on her way to the stairs. I hear her bedroom door close a minute later.

I shake my head. "I'm sorry, I don't understand."

"I'm your date."

"Jed," I sigh.

He steps forward. "I know it's crazy, but somewhere through all of this, I fell for you. And I know I've hurt you in the past, but I want to make up for that. I don't deserve a second chance, but I'm asking for one anyway because I can't live without you."

I sigh again.

He takes another step toward me. "Just hear me out. I know I have Emilia and you don't ever want a relationship or probably to be a stepmom, but can we just explore this and see where it can go? Maybe you'll change your mind."

"Stepmom?" What is he talking about?

"I know. I know." He shakes his head. "But am I really the only one who felt this connection deepen between us?" He reaches for my hand.

I let him take it, the warmth from his fingers spreading up my arm. "I heard you last night with Emilia, saying something about me not ever being her mom."

He rears his head back and his eyes widen. "I think you

misunderstood. I figured *you* didn't want that, so I didn't want Emilia to get her hopes up. I didn't want her to get invested only to be heartbroken if that was something you'd never be up for."

"At first, I didn't think I would want that, mostly because of my insecurities."

He breaks the distance between us and places his hand on my cheek, then gently urges me to look at him. "You said I was different from the other guys before. What did you mean?"

I shake my head, trying to keep my emotions in. Oh hell, what does it matter at this point? "It was always you, Jed. You were the one I always wanted, but you were unavailable."

"Emotionally yes, but that's all changed." He stares at me as if he's willing me to feel his next words. "I'm in love with you, Molly. I'm so in love with you that I don't know what I'll do if you turn me away right now."

His confession bowls me over. I want to ask if he's sure and double- and triple-check, but he's right. I've felt it these last few weeks too. Which is why I was so crushed by what I overheard the other night. I'd thought we were building something together, even if we hadn't discussed it.

"I love you too."

I wish I had a camera to capture his smile.

"I'm pretty irresistible, right? Especially with Emilia now." I laugh and shove his chest, but he doesn't move. He circles his arm around my waist and pulls me flush into him. "Will you go on a date with me?"

"Okay, but no sleeping together."

His palm cradles my cheek and his thumb drags down until it's lightly stroking my chin. "You can make the rules, but is kissing allowed?"

He's already bending toward me and I'm inching up on my toes. "Definitely."

Our lips meet in the gentlest kiss he's ever given me, as though he's trying to tell me everything in this one kiss. My gut says this is right. This is perfect. This is where I need to be.

He closes the kiss, resting his forehead on mine, and we both find our breath again. His fingers slide down my arm until he secures my hand in his and guides me out of the house. We walk to his truck, and he opens the passenger door for me.

"Hmm…" I say.

He tilts his head. "Seriously?"

I kiss his cheek and climb into the passenger seat. He shuts the door and rounds the front of the truck before climbing in.

Before he starts the ignition, he leans over and kisses me. "Just so you know, that's your permanent seat now."

I smile at him, full of joy. "Deal."

Epilogue

Jed

Five months later...

$\mathcal{E}$milia claps when Presley finishes reading the fairy tale about a prince and a princess at her small bookstore, The Story Shop. I'm not too keen on my daughter thinking she needs any type of boy in her life, especially one to save her. I'm teaching her to do that for herself. But Presley seems big on fairy tales these days— probably because she's living her own, as evidenced by the flash of her wedding ring when she closes the book.

She and Cade are finally married, and now I can finally enjoy Cade working like he should. The funny thing is, now I'm the one pushing us back on some of the advances I've always wanted the company to take because I want to spend time with Molly and Emilia.

"Did you like it?" Presley asks Emilia.

"Yeah," Emilia answers with a smile.

"Tell me your favorite part," Presley says, taking Emilia's hand and walking away from the story area.

My daughter babbles on as though she's been talking her entire life, and I couldn't be prouder.

"I'm starving." Molly wraps her arms around my waist. "Are you going to feed me?"

"I don't think that's appropriate in front of the children."

She smacks my back and sighs.

"Yeah, we'll go next door, but not yet. We're meeting Simone."

Her eyes light up. "You didn't tell me that. Did something come on the market?"

I would've loved to buy a house for Molly and Emilia—wrapped up a key and say, "Surprise, welcome home,"—but I'm not an idiot, no matter what people say. Molly needs this process as much as I do. She needs to look at houses and get that feeling of home. So we've been looking, but it's hard to get a house under contract fast enough right now. With the Bailey Lumber Company expanding in the area, they've brought in more workers, which means the housing market kind of boomed.

"It did and she got us an early showing, but if we like it, we have to put in the offer today."

She slides out of my hold and grabs my hand. "Let's go. Emilia!"

I chuckle and pull her back to me. "Relax. We have some time."

"Babe, I know you don't mind living with Fisher. You two can play video games and you're getting that bachelor life while getting laid regularly, but I can't do it anymore. I'm done with getting dressed in a steamy bathroom when he's home and the family movie nights that get interrupted. He's great and Emilia's going to miss him like crazy, but I need out."

I laugh at her again and push her hair behind her ear. "I know, and believe me, I do want our own place. Especially one with a master bed and bath so you can just walk out of the bathroom naked after a shower. I promise to lotion you up."

She looks around like someone might overhear us, but she knows she'd like it too.

"I'm hungry." Emilia comes over to us.

I swoop her up in my arms. She turns four tomorrow, and maybe it's weird, but I already feel her asserting her independence from me.

"Let's go. Thanks, Presley," I say, holding my hand up in a wave.

Molly and Emilia say goodbye too, and we walk out onto the cobblestone streets of Sunrise Bay. As we walk, I explain to Emilia that we'll eat in a little bit, but first we're going to go look at a house.

I catch sight of my mom and Hank taking down the "Greene for Mayor" signs. My heart sinks because my mom ended up losing when Sam Klein decided he wasn't going to retire after all. And he's done such a great job with Sunrise Bay that it was a tough decision for people to make.

"Maybe if she saw Emilia, it would cheer her up?" Molly suggests, but we're on a tight schedule.

"She'll see her tomorrow. Plus, Hank will take care of her."

We continue to the other edge of downtown, closer to where Cade and Presley live. At least if this house pans out, we'll live by them.

My phone rings in my pocket and I pull it out, then seeing it's my dad, I send it to voice mail. With Molly's encouragement, we've spoken a couple of times since Emilia's arrival, but he's yet to meet his granddaughter which is fine by me. We can carry on a conversation if need be but I don't want him involved in our lives in any big way.

Next thing we know, we're standing outside a cute two-story steel-blue house with a wraparound porch and a white picket fence around the front yard.

"This looks too nice for us," Molly says.

I take her hand. "No such thing."

Our realtor, Simone, greets us and opens the door the minute we step on the porch. It has a swing and everything.

Did I ever think I would live here? Hell no. This isn't my style, but I do love the fact it looks like a home.

Molly steps inside with Emilia at her side.

"Go check the bedrooms," Simone whispers to Emilia.

Emilia looks back to us for permission before running up the stairs.

I can't tell if Molly likes the house or not. We've already been disappointed a few times, so she keeps up a front now whenever we look at a house. Thinking we found the house for us only to be outbid by someone else has led to nothing but disappointment.

But at least her career is going well. She started as the speech pathologist for the school board in our area, so she works with kids in Sunrise Bay, Greywall, and Lake Starlight elementary schools.

I follow Molly through the house, and Simone nudges me as if I can sense what Molly's thinking. We haven't been together that long, and though I'm getting closer, I'm not quite there yet. We reach the kitchen. It's newly remodeled, which I know Molly loves but won't admit. She has a hard time admitting she loves things because she still fears losing them. Which I'm working on day by day.

After we're done looking at the downstairs—which has a great layout, if you ask me—Molly takes the stairs one at a time, inspecting everything. Emilia runs down the hall to meet us at the top of the stairs.

"Mommy, come." She grabs Molly's hand and drags her.

This was a tough one to navigate. Molly and I are in agreement that we will not be getting married. We're happy together as is, and neither of us feels the need for a piece of paper to prove that to anyone. At first, we had Emilia call her Molly, but Mommy just kept coming out and we figure why try to change it? Molly is a permanent fixture in our lives, marriage license or not.

I returned to Minnesota and completed all the paperwork. I was somewhat relieved when David told me he did a more exhaustive search for family members but didn't find anything. It would've been nice to have people who could tell Emilia stories about her mother, but I'm relieved I won't have to worry about someone popping up and thinking they can do a better job with my daughter than I can. But we do have the Webbs, who are coming out next summer. Weird how things work out.

"You're never going to believe this," Molly says from one of the bedrooms. "Jed!"

Simone and I make our way down the hall, and I see it before I'm even in the room. The room is painted neon orange, all four walls and the ceiling.

Emilia presses her body to the wall with her arms out to her sides. "I love it!"

Molly and I look at one another. "We'll take it," we say in unison.

The next day

We got the house! Mostly because Simone knew the sellers, I think, but whatever. We close in thirty days, which means we only have to live with Fisher for thirty more days. He's not a horrible roommate, but we need space for ourselves. He offered to leave, but this is his family home. He should be here.

Since it's Emilia's fourth birthday, we're throwing a party at my mom and Hank's place. It's fall, so Hank set up the firepit and we're all bundled in coats and pants, but the sun is out, which makes it a little warmer.

I sit at the table and remember months ago when I was here for the summer bash and thought my life was lost.

I look at Molly holding Noah, Nikki and Logan's newborn. She's a natural and doesn't even know it. She sways like a mom. I hope one day she wants to have kids so we can experience this from day one together. Then the baby gets fussy, and since Nikki's a little overprotective, she practically snatches the baby out of Molly's arms before she has a chance to soothe him.

Molly comes and sits on my lap since our seating is restricted now that our family is so large. We watch Emilia play with Lucy and Adam's foster son, Alex. He's two years older and tends to goad my daughter into doing dangerous things. We found them in a tree last weekend, and I didn't even want to know how they managed to get so far up. Those two are trouble together.

From what I hear, Adam and Lucy are getting ready to start in vitro. I hope they're successful.

Molly follows my vision to Emilia and Alex messing around. "Relax, they're fine."

"He's always getting her to do risky stuff."

Molly laughs and kisses my cheek, pressing her breasts to my side. "You've done a one-eighty."

I have, and having her in my lap is proof of that. What was I ever thinking avoiding this before?

I'm lost in my thoughts, my hand running along the small of her back, so she's the first one to react when Emilia screams. Molly runs toward her and I follow right behind.

"What happened?" Molly asks.

Adam and Lucy rush over too.

"I swear I didn't do anything," Alex says, clearly in a panic. "I swear."

Lucy takes him in her arms and soothes him while he cries.

"I think we have to take her in. It might be broken," Molly says.

"Broken? What?" I yell, coming up beside Molly to see Emilia's arm not looking quite normal. "Does it hurt?"

Emilia shakes her head and tears well in her eyes. "I tripped on that stick."

I look over and see a large stick in the deadening grass, then I pick her up. Molly helps me make sure her arm is in a good place.

"I'm sorry, Emilia," Alex says.

"It's okay. She'll be fine. It was just an accident," I reassure him. I'll be honest, it takes a lot for me not to lay into him, but I know kids have accidents all the time. It's a part of growing up.

"We'll meet them at the hospital. It's okay," Lucy tells Alex.

An hour later, Emilia's in an emergency room bed, and sure enough, she broke her arm. But it was a clean break, so they'll cast it and it should heal just fine.

Once Emilia's in good shape—eating a popsicle, thanks to the nurses—I leave her and Molly in search of a vending machine before my stomach eats itself. Most of the family has gone home. We might meet them back over at the house once it's casted, depending on how long it takes.

"Allie. We've missed you!" a nurse says, which draws my attention to the right.

Sure enough, it's Allie. I haven't seen her around in so long that I've wondered what happened between her and Fisher, but I didn't ask because it was clear he didn't want to discuss it.

"Thanks. Stella really needed me over at her practice for a while until she could find a suitable replacement for her nurse who left. I got lucky that you were so short-staffed that you wanted me back since she's finally found someone who works." She takes off her coat and I blink. Twice.

Oh, fuck.

I rush back into Emilia's room. She's watching some Disney movie and Molly's flipping through a magazine.

Molly asks, "Did you find something to eat?"

"Come here." I grab Molly's arm and drag her to the door.

"What's wrong with you?"

"Just look out the door. Remember Allie? Fisher's friend?"

"Vaguely." She peers out the door and comes back with her mouth gaping. Then she counts on her fingers and her mouth widens even more.

"I should go say something, right?" I ask. "Like, congratulate her and see if she seems weird because it's Fisher's baby, but he clearly *doesn't know*."

She shoots me a look like I'm crazy. "You never congratulate a woman unless you know for sure she's pregnant."

"She's clearly with child," I say.

"With child? Did you just escape from Northern Lights?"

I pull out my phone and she snatches it away.

"This is none of our business," she says.

"Fisher needs to know. There's definitely a possibility it could be his." I look at Allie again. Sure enough, she's rubbing her small baby bump the way I watched Nikki do over and over again.

Molly hands my phone back to me. "Shit. I guess so."

Me: *You been to the hospital lately?*

Fisher: *Hey I heard what happened, stopped to get her something. I'm almost there.*

He wasn't at the birthday party because he was working. A strangled noise comes out of me.

"What?" Molly asks, eyes wide.

"He's going to be here soon." I cringe.

She pushes me toward the door. "Go meet him. You have to give him a heads-up."

I look both ways, no longer seeing Allie, so I head out to meet Fisher by the entrance of the emergency room.

Sure enough, his truck pulls up and he's got a balloon bouquet in his hand. "Can you believe all they had at the store were congratulations balloons? But I figure she'd love the balloons anyway, right?"

My heart beats faster the closer he gets, and a cold sweat sprinkles my forehead.

"How is she? Why are you so pale? Did something happen? Is it serious?" he asks in rapid-fire fashion.

"She's fine. It's a broken arm."

He makes a face and walks into the emergency room

without me. He says hello to the nurse on duty, who bites her lip. Does she know too?

I head inside, knowing I should tell him, but I have no idea how.

"What room is Emilia in?" Fisher glances over his shoulder at me.

I spot Allie down the hall, her shoes coming to a loud squeaking stop. Fisher spots her and stops as well. It's like a standoff, and my breath lodges in my throat.

"What the fuck?" he murmurs.

"Fisher," Allie says, clearly surprised to see him.

Molly comes to the door that's directly between them.

"What the hell is going on?" Fisher asks.

Allie puts her hand on her stomach, and my eyes widen at Molly. Fisher hands the bouquet of balloons to me and approaches Allie, gently taking her elbow and leading her right into Emilia's room. I follow because I'm nosy and Molly and Emilia are in there anyway.

"What is that?" Fisher asks, pointing at Allie's belly.

"A baby," she says with attitude.

"Whose baby?" He enunciates each syllable as though she maybe doesn't speak English.

Even Emilia is staring.

"Yours."

The room is silent.

"Baby!" Emilia exclaims.

I hand the bouquet of balloons back to Fisher. "Looks like these are for you after all."

The End

The Baileys

Lessons from a One-Night Stand (FREE)

Advice from a Jilted Bride

Birth of a Baby Daddy

Operation Bailey Wedding (Novella)

Falling for My Brother's Best Friend

Demise of a Self-Centered Playboy

Confessions of a Naughty Nanny

Operation Bailey Babies (Novella)

Secrets of the World's Worst Matchmaker

Winning my Best Friend's Girl

Rules for Dating Your Ex

Operation Bailey Birthday (Novella)

The Greene Family

My Twist of Fortune (Free Prequel)

My Beautiful Neighbor (FREE)

My Almost Ex

My Vegas Groom

A Greene Family Summer Bash (Novella)

My Sister's Flirty Friend

My Unexpected Surprise

My Famous Frenemy

A Greene Family Vacation (Novella)

My Scorned Best Friend

My Fake Fiancé

My Brother's Forbidden Friend

A Greene Family Christmas (Novella)

Lake Starlight

The Problem with Second Chances

The Issue with Bad Boy Roommates

The Trouble with Runaway Brides

The Drawback of Single Dads

Plain Daisy Ranch

One Last Summer

The One I Left Behind

The One I Stood Beside

The One I Didn't See Coming

Modern Love

Charmed by the Bartender

Hooked by the Boxer

Mad about the Banker

Single Dads Club

Real Deal

Dirty Talker

Sexy Beast

Hollywood Hearts

Mister Mom

Animal Attraction

Domestic Bliss

Bedroom Games

Cold as Ice

On Thin Ice

Break the Ice

Chicago Law

Smitten with the Best Man

Tempted by my Ex-Husband

Seduced by my Ex's Divorce Attorney

Blue Collar Brothers

Flirting with Fire

Crushing on the Cop

Engaged to the EMT

White Collar Brothers

Sexy Filthy Boss

Dirty Flirty Enemy

Wild Steamy Hook-up

The Rooftop Crew

My Bestie's Ex

A Royal Mistake

The Rival Roomies

Our Star-Crossed Kiss

The Do-Over

A Co-Workers Crush

Hockey Hotties

Countdown to a Kiss (Free Prequel)

My Lucky #13 (FREE)

The Trouble with #9

Faking it with #41

Tropical Hat Trick (Novella)

Sneaking around with #34

Second Shot with #76

Offside with #55

Kingsmen Football Stars

False Start (Free Prequel)

You Had Your Chance, Lee Burrows

You Can't Kiss the Nanny, Brady Banks

Over My Brother's Dead Body, Chase Andrews

Chicago Grizzlies

On the Defense (Free Prequel)

Something like Hate

Something like Lust

Something like Love

The Nest

Mr. Heartbreaker

Mr. Broody

Mr. S (Title to be revealed)

Mr. C (Title to be revealed)

Holiday Romances

Single and Ready to Jingle

Claus and Effect

Merry Kissmas

Cockamamie Unicorn Ramblings

It's so great to be back with the Greene family! Jed. Jed. Jed. He was a hard one to figure out. When we wrote the ending of the Greene Family Summer Bash novella it kind of just came out that Molly was calling off an affair with Jed. But we went with it because it felt right. That made us change their story a little from our original idea so that we could go back in time to show you how they became lovers in the first place.

Rayne doesn't always do well having to write back in time mostly because she hates figuring out the timeline and this book proved no different. Add on some vacations between both of us and Rayne's kids going back to school and let's just say we're lucky we hit the deadline.

At one point, an aunt was going to come into the picture and threaten to take Emilia away from Jed, but it turned out the part with Emilia calling Molly Mama felt like enough and doing anything more felt like unnecessary drama for this could. They had enough drama early on anyway, right? They deserved their happily ever after!

As always we have a lot of people to thank for getting this book into your hands…

- Danielle Sanchez and the entire Wildfire Marketing Solutions team.

- Cassie from Joy Editing for line edits.
- Ellie from My Brother's Editor for line edits.
- Rosa from My Brother's Editor for proofreading.
- Hang Le for the cover and branding for the entire series.
- Wander Aguiar for his awesome job of photographing our Nikki and Logan.
- Bloggers who consistently carve out time to read, review and/or promote us.
- Piper Rayne Unicorns who are our safe place in this crazy world!
- Readers who took the time to read our story when there's so many choices out there.

Next up, Fisher and Allie who you may remember first appeared in Winning my Best Friend's Girl (Bailey #8). We've been impatiently waiting to see Allie hit the page in her own book and she could not be paired with a more perfect hero than our broody Sheriff Greene. Surprise pregnancy anyone! :P

xo,

Piper & Rayne

About Piper & Rayne

Piper Rayne is a USA Today Bestselling Author duo who write "heartwarming humor with a side of sizzle" about families, whether that be blood or found. They both have e-readers full of one-clickable books, they're married to husbands who drive them to drink, and they're both chauffeurs to their kids. Most of all, they love hot heroes and quirky heroines who make them laugh, and they hope you do, too!

www.ingramcontent.com/pod-product-compliance
Lightning Source LLC
Chambersburg PA
CBHW021156010826
48971CB00014B/2190